A Heart that Dances

J.P. STERLING

Contents

Chapter One

As I walked briskly through Paris' residential streets on my way home, I was mesmerized to see a transparent frost had blanketed the city, instantly freezing the autumn foliage with moisture that shimmered in the moonlight. The sudden shift in seasons reminded me of when I was a little girl—still filled with a foolish and overactive imagination—and how I used to imagine that ballerinas brought about the shift in seasons. I'm sure it was because I watched entirely too many Nutcracker and Sleeping Beauty ballets. The world of Tchaikovsky forever embedded into my brain that beautiful dancing princesses were the center of everything. It's silly now, but to a six-year-old girl it was only logical that I would think ballerinas were part of the natural law. I imagined them dancing in the spring meadows, and as they twirled, newly budded flowers sprinkled out everywhere around them, seeding the bare lands. If you were lucky enough, you would occasionally see a butterfly unfold from a rare rainbow swirl or even more extraordinary, a bubbling waterfall that also brought baskets of newborn puppies and kitties floating to their new homes.

Then as the weather evolved into a chilly autumn, the ballerinas would return to dance on top of the blooming flowers, signaling them to close and go to sleep. However, the ballerinas were at their most brilliant in winter when they came to bring in the frost by vigorously twirling, stirring up a wind spiral that grew until it was a glistening white tornado that frosted everything in its path.

They would, of course, always come unannounced and dance in secret. It had been my fantasy to spot them by stealing random, midnight looks outside my bedroom window when I could hear the winds howl. I continually looked for evidence of their tiny footprints in my yard. In my little-girl mind, tonight would have been one of those nights the ballerinas had clandestinely danced, frosting all the things. I smiled to myself when I thought about how innocent I had been. In a way, I sort of missed the days when weather-changing ballerinas made sense.

My phone vibrated inside my pocket, startling me out of my daydream, but I was quickly calmed when I saw who it was. "Hey, Fulton."

"Well . . . tell me," he immediately pressed. "How did it go?"

"Did you watch it online?"

"I did."

"What did you think?"

"I couldn't see much. I saw your model walk out at the end of Gabby's showcase. She didn't trip or anything so I'm assuming that's good. What did you think?"

"I thought it was surreal." I chuckled lightly, not because it was humorous but because I had a giddiness inside that I needed to let out. "I honestly can't even describe it. I didn't know what to expect. All day my stomach was a wreck but then it was over in what felt like two seconds."

"I figured you had to be dying somewhere backstage."

"I was," I agreed. "But then the coolest thing happened!"

"What was that?"

"As soon as the show was over, I was backstage with the models and Gabby. Reporters were everywhere trying to get interviews with the models and designers. I was squeezing my way through the crowd when I bumped into a fashion reporter who somehow recognized me, and she asked to interview *me*."

"For real?"

"Yes! I didn't think that would even be a thing, so I didn't know what to say. She caught me completely off-guard."

"What did you say?"

"She asked me about the inspiration behind my dress. I explained I had a passion for styles that highlighted modern trends with a nod toward a vintage-inspired femininity."

"Oh, that sounds fancy."

"I know! My dad helped me come up with that elevator pitch a few months ago. I was so thankful he did because honestly that's all I had."

"Well, of course he would make you do that." Fulton's supportive chuckle flowed through the phone. "Then what happened?"

"I shared the story about how I found that vintage Dior dress in a trunk at a friend's attic, and how I knew I wanted to design fashion that felt royal to the everyday woman."

"What did she say then?"

"Nothing really. The interview went fast. Now that I think of it, it might have been more of a pity interview while she waited to get time with Gabby, but it was super cool to be able to share my work with all those people."

"I doubt it was a pity interview," Fulton said. "And I'm glad everything turned out well."

"It did. I mean, it was stressful to get to this point, but it was worth it."

"What did Gabby say?"

"I didn't get to talk to her. She had so much press to get through that she left to make her rounds after the show. I stayed to help clean up and do all the things free labor gets roped into doing."

"See, I knew you'd be amazing. You were so stressed, but everything was awesome. I wish I could have been there to see you."

"Thanks. I wish you could have been here too . . . but not just for the show." I lowered lashes to the ground. "I miss you."

"I miss you too. I wish we could be together," he said in a quieter voice. Then he added, "It's how it needs to be right now while we are both chasing our dreams, but it'll work out and be worth it."

"I hope so. And if this doesn't work out for me here, my next dream is going to have to at least be on the same continent as you are."

"Deal," Fulton agreed.

"Oh, and by the way, thank you for the flowers you sent. They are beautiful."

"You're welcome."

"So, what are you doing now?" I asked.

"I'm actually walking home too."

"Did you go out?"

"Yeah, a few of us went to see some weird show at the theatre."

"Why was it weird?"

"I don't really know how to describe it. I mean, I'm all for supporting the arts and what Wally's trying to do now that he has taken over managing the theatre for his dad. I don't know if he's struggling to get talent booked, but it was a strange play where all the characters were played by the same person, which actually sounded cool, and it should have been, but the plot was beyond odd."

"How so?"

"It's hard to explain but it was like each character had their own solo show, and they didn't seem interconnected. But it was fine. A night off from studying for me." After a brief pause, Fulton picked up the conversation again. "So, now that your show is over and you've had an opportunity to reap some rewards, do you think this fashion stuff is the right path?"

I took a deep breath and let it out slowly. "I think so. It seems like all the doors are opening in that direction. I might as well walk through them."

"That seems sort of nonchalant for you." His voice held an air of suspicion. "You usually aren't that calm."

I arrived at my apartment building, but I loitered outside, needing another moment to savor the night air. "Oh, trust me, I've been there. I've felt all the emotions but right now I feel good. I love working with Gabby, and I love my life here in Paris and getting to meet all these amazing people. There is nothing else I would want to be doing differently career-wise. Today happened and now I keep moving forward to see what happens next."

"Well, I'm positive it will go well for you."

"I guess I'll have to see," I said, then I changed the subject. "When do you fly out?"

"First thing in the morning. I should be in Montana by noon."

"That's early. I have an early flight too, but I won't be in Virginia by noon."

"You should have lots of time to rest on the plane then."

"I hope I can sleep. It's going to be great to do nothing."

"I agree. I'm ready for a break too."

"Well, I hate to let you go but it's super late, and I'm standing outside because I don't want to wake up my neighbors, but it's cold here."

"Oh, I'm sorry. You should have said. I'll let you go."

"Can you keep me updated on how your flights and everything go tomorrow?"

"Sure."

"Okay. Good night then. Talk to you soon."

"Good night."

I ended the call. This day had been too busy, too exciting, and too everything. I hadn't even had time to process what had actually happened. *Gabby had talked me into showing a dress I had designed by myself in a fashion show, and everything was successful!* My life was perfect insanity right now. Never in a million years would I think I would get the chance to move to Paris and pursue my dream of becoming a designer and to have everything go so smoothly—it was a dream come true!

I reluctantly pulled on the heavy wooden door with my free hand as I stole a final glimpse at the trees now dipped in frost. I smirked at my foolishness, but then I let my eyes dance over the silvery grass, seeking anything that looked like it had been touched by ballerinas. A whimsical smile pooled in the corner of my lips until I couldn't resist it anymore. Maybe, weather-changing ballerinas didn't really exist but they were symbolic of all the good things that were great that we couldn't see, like dreams. Tonight, they were reminding me to believe in all the good that is unseen.

Chapter Two

Flight delay notifications chimed on my phone before I even opened my eyes. I grimaced, remembering I had to fly to my parents' house today. I don't think anybody could have dragged their feet more than I did as I tried to come up with any excuse to stay home. *Maybe I need to walk the dog . . . that I don't have. Or shovel the snow . . . that my landlord already cleared. I could clean out my fridge . . . that was mostly empty anyway.* I sighed heavily, feeling both my obligation and my defeat. Then I reluctantly stuffed extra clothes into my dance bag.

When I finally arrived at the airport, my pessimistic mood still hadn't peaked. I sulked even more when I saw an updated airport screen flash a new flight time, adding *another* hour to my already delayed departure time. "Great," I muttered to no one. If I'd known I would have this much time to kill, I would have stayed home longer. Now I was stuck here with nothing to do. I pulled out my phone to call Fulton.

"Hey," he answered.

"Hey, they added another hour to my departure time. I think they are trying to wait out the blizzards in the U.S." I glanced out the window to see light gray clouds but no new moisture. "It's done snowing here."

"I guess that's what you get for waiting to visit until Thanksgiving. You're bound to have a snowstorm somewhere."

I crossed my free arm over my chest and huffed. I hated wasting all this time. "Are you snowed in?"

"Not snowed in, but we have the usual foot of snow for Montana."

"Is it weird to be back?"

"Nah, it's only for a few days, but who knows"— his voice lifted, hinting of teasing— "I may decide I've been missing this place and want to move back."

The airport screen flashed, updating again, adding another twenty minutes to my delayed departure. "You're kidding," I grumbled. "They delayed me again—another twenty minutes." I turned my back to the flight screen and went to look out the window. "I don't know. Maybe I should skip it. I mean, I was only going to be there for three days. With all the delays, by the time I get there, it'll feel like no time before I have to do this all over again." Then I added, "What if I get stuck? Gabby has a huge holiday event she needs me for next week. She'd die if I didn't make it back to help her."

"You won't get stuck," Fulton reassured me. "You need to visit your parents. It's Thanksgiving."

"Not in Europe. It wouldn't bother me one bit to stay here. It's such a big hassle to fly this time of year, and you know how my parents are. It's not like we ever hang out."

"It seems like a hassle now, but it'll be worth it." His voice was slightly urgent, which seemed off because he normally left a boundary when talking about my family issues. "You need to go visit them."

"Why?" I felt defensive. "They could just as easily come see me. Actually, it would be easier for them to visit me since they're retired. I'm over here working fifty hours a week and have a super tight schedule."

"You've been working nonstop," Fulton agreed. "Your parents understand you're busy. They probably don't want to impose, but the fact that you've been working nonstop is another reason to take a few days off so you can have a break to regroup." When I didn't say anything, he echoed, "And again, it's Thanksgiving, and they're your *parents*."

My brow lowered while I wondered why he cared so much. My parents weren't in Montana anymore. It's not like I would get to see him too. He usually didn't take an opinion on stuff like that. I glared at the screen, which had thankfully not updated again. "Well, since I'm here, I might as well stay," I huffed.

"You'll be glad you did."

Something about his position on this visit still bothered me but I couldn't place why. After a moment, I decided it was probably just my annoyance with the delays. "Well, I'll let you go. I'm scoping out some strong coffee."

"Okay, sounds good. Keep me updated."

After I paid for coffee, I remembered I still needed to update my parents on my flight changes. I reluctantly pressed the send button on my dad's phone number. It wasn't that I didn't want to talk to them. It was more that things had gotten weird since they moved back east to be closer to my mom's sister, Kim. They had thought it would help my mom to move past her perpetual state of depression, but as it always had been, things stayed the same. Well, maybe a little better. My mom was able to stay at the condo this time with my dad but only because she was leaving almost daily for therapy or group meetings.

Whenever I talked to my dad, he never mentioned my aunt. I doubt they even see her. It never made sense to make their last move, but I didn't dwell on it, because nothing they did ever made sense to me. It was almost as if they would write out a bunch of random and irrational things they could do on slips of paper and then dump them into a hat to randomly draw one out and say, "Yep, that's it. We'll do that next."

So, now my dad went back to work full time, consulting to make extra money to fund all of my mom's treatment. I can't complain because he pays for my bills while I worked for free with Gabby—which was probably the only reason that I hadn't turned around to head back to my apartment. I needed my dad's financial support. I listened to the phone ring until it went to voicemail and then I hung up. "Hmm, that's strange he didn't answer," I thought, but my thoughts were quickly interrupted by an in-coming call from Gabby. "Hey!" I greeted her with enthusiasm.

"Hey! I was freaking out here at the office, waiting for you to come in so we could scream about last night, but then I remembered you were on vacation, so I had to call. How are you?"

"I'm still in total disbelief." I held the front of my chest to feel my heart accelerate. "I know it was basically nothing, but nothing would have never happened if it wasn't for you pushing me—"

"Supporting you," Gabby cut in.

"Supporting me," I agreed. "I'm extremely grateful you put up with me and . . ." I shook my head as I struggled to come up with the right words. "I—I just need to say thank you," I finally managed.

"You're welcome," Gabby stated like a proud mama. "It was a blast to see everything go well for both of us."

"It did go well for both of us," I agreed. "I've never seen you have that kind of reception before."

"I don't know if I've ever had that many requests for interviews and photos," Gabby said. "Paris is definitely a whole different game than New York."

"I'd say," I agreed. "It's so worth it."

"I think so too," Gabby said. "So, does that mean you're glad you made the move?"

"Of course, I am. There isn't anything I would rather be doing. To be honest, I'd rather work this weekend than fly back to the States, but I figured I have to visit my folks so they keep funding me."

"Yes," Gabby said, her voice lowering, "you do need to make sure you keep your relationships healthy."

"I wish it wasn't such a long flight," I complained.

"Enjoy it, because when you get back, I'm going to work your butt off."

I chortled, knowing she wasn't even a little bit kidding. "I'm sure you will."

"I am. I signed us both up for a spring show, so you have a little over three months to get ready."

"What do you mean *us*?"

"You'll have your own showcase with your own models to dress."

I felt my jaw lower. "Ah, what?"

"You might as well take advantage of the opportunity while you are here. Your dad isn't going to support you forever. We want your resume to be loaded and your portfolio to be packed by the end of this year. Lots of exposure too."

I didn't know what to say. Gabby was one of those people who was naturally caffeinated, thriving on chaos to push herself closer to her goals. I wasn't like that. I preferred to over-prepare and agonize about details. Her confidence in my ability to dress multiple models in a few months felt terrifyingly premature. However, I didn't want to say anything to appear ungrateful. More than that, I was horrified of screwing this up and disappointing her.

She must have sensed my anxiety, because she added, "I'm going to help you every step of the way. Don't worry. We're going to do this together."

I swallowed hard, already starting to feel the budding pressure in my gut. "Promise?"

"Of course. That's what I'm here for."

"I'm glad you cleared that up, because I was beginning to think you were in my life to increase my odds of dying from an anxiety attack."

She laughed and then added, "Nah, that's just what being an adult is all about."

"I don't like it."

"You get used to it, and it can be fun. Speaking of which, I suppose I need to get to work, but I wanted you to know how proud I was of you. Thank you for all your work on my showcase too. I've never had this much success or fun."

"It is fun, isn't it?" I confessed.

"Crazy fun."

"You're welcome and thank you for your support. I'll try to take it easy for the next couple of days and then you can torture me when I get back next week."

"Deal."

As I ended the call, my face was frozen in a perpetual grin, and I immediately started to text Fulton about Gabby's new scheme for my spring showcase. I didn't have a clue how I was going to be ready by then, but I trusted Gabby when she said she would help me. I was fast becoming addicted to the thrill of fashion.

It was almost twenty-four hours later when I stepped off my plane into the Richmond airport. I breezed past bag check with no need to stop for luggage claim since I had learned to travel with only a carryon bag. I checked my phone for an update from my dad while scanning the passenger pickup lane at the same time. I didn't see any texts. I also didn't notice any vehicles with my dad in them. "I can't believe I am even surprised by this." I sighed heavily. "Like, seriously," I continued, muttering under my breath as I walked briskly down the pickup lane, looking for my dad, "never in my life have I ever heard of parents who constantly lack the courtesy to be present for their child." I opened my text messages again, and still nothing! I didn't waste any time in sending a text to my dad:

"Hey, Dad! Did you forget something? I can't believe you can't even meet me at the airport. Oh wait, I can believe that you would ditch me again. What I can't believe is that I fell for this again. I should have stayed home. I don't deserve this treatment!"

I pushed send quickly before I lost my nerve. Then I glared at my phone screen, waiting for it to light up with my dad's number and some lame excuse about how my mom was going nuts and that's why he wasn't here, again. But nothing happened.

I rubbed my tired eyes and tried not to scream. I couldn't believe I was giving them another chance; I didn't want to, but my return flight wasn't for a couple of days. I needed somewhere to stay. I opened my browser to search for a ride share number when I heard a woman's voice call my name. With suspicious eyes, I stared at a lady sitting in a car in the passenger pickup lane. Her left elbow was resting on her opened window while she leaned out, looking right at me, waving to get my attention. Noticing she looked a lot like my mom, I determined it had to be my mom's sister, Kim, and I walked over to her. "Let me guess, my dad sent you to pick me up because he couldn't make it."

She motioned to the passenger seat. "Yeah, hop in."

I focused on taking measured breaths. Now relieved that at least *someone* was here, I was quickly becoming resentful for being ditched again. After climbing into the car, I clicked my seatbelt, then waited for whatever epic excuse my dad had this time.

"How are you?" Kim asked, obviously trying to make small talk, but I wasn't into it.

"I'm not sure," I said a little bitterly.

"That's fair," Kim said. "So, this is going to appear sort of crazy, but I'm here because your dad is in the hospital."

"He never said anything to me." Unconvinced, I glanced at my phone and scrolled through my messages again, looking for one that I may have missed. "Is he okay?"

"He collapsed this morning when he tried to get out of bed . . ."

My chin tilted toward her, but she didn't expand on any details. I was cautious because I didn't know Kim. I treaded lightly. "Is he sick?"

She pulled the car forward out of the parking lane and turned onto the street. "I'll take you over there, and you can see for yourself."

"Okay," I agreed. Then I had another thought. I hadn't heard from either parent. "Is my mom with him?"

She glanced briefly at me before returning her eyes to the road. "I wish I wouldn't have to be the one to tell you all this stuff. Can you wait until we get to the hospital?"

Her diversion confirmed what I had already known—that my mom wasn't well—but that confused me because I thought Kim was supposed to help take care of her. "Are you helping with her?"

"Well, no." She chuckled lightly but not in a humorous way, more like how you laugh when you are avoiding something. "She doesn't like me enough to let me care for her."

I pursed my lips, reflecting on how my mom had hated Kim, but that brought up my uneasiness about how I never felt right about the reasons my parents had given me as to why they moved here in the first place. I knew my mom's situation well enough to know she wasn't absent from picking me up because she was at the hospital taking care of my dad. If she didn't come to pick me up, then something wasn't right with her. "Is she in a treatment home again?" I asked.

"You ask a lot of questions."

"I just know how she is." My voice was flat and unbothered when I looked at her with a sideways glance. "You can tell me the truth. I can handle it."

"She's in the state hospital."

"Really?" I asked quietly. My eyebrows lifted, but my heart sank with guilt. I had no idea that she had been *that* sick. My dad never put her in those types of places. Something must have been drastically wrong for my dad to do that! "Do you know she hates hospitals like that?"

"Well, she wasn't happy about it, but your dad was unable to care for her, and she hates me. I didn't have a choice."

"Why couldn't my dad help?" Now things were really getting weird. My dad ditched me all the time, but he was always there for my mom. Always.

"I'll let him explain it to you."

I lightly chewed on the inside of my cheek. This went against everything my dad had fought for his whole life. "Wasn't there something local that would have been more comfortable?"

"I don't know." She threw one of her hands up in the air like she was giving up. "I did what I had to do. I work fulltime and have kids, so I can't be running after her. Plus, all those other homes are expensive, and I don't have that kind of money. This seemed like the best option for right now."

"So, you put her there?" Maybe I should have been used to how confusing my parents were, but I could tell by her vague and rushed comment that there was something big she wasn't revealing to me.

"I signed her in. Your dad gave me power over her healthcare."

This was getting crazier by the minute. Something wasn't adding up. "Well, how's she doing there?"

"I'm sure she's fine."

The exhaustion in her tone gave her away because it was the same tone I used when people asked me that question about my mom. I instantly knew she had been avoiding my mom, but I wasn't angry. In a way, I understood her forced blithe. I lowered my voice and asked, "It's too hard to visit her, isn't it?"

With a stolid expression, she agreed. "Impossible at times."

Even though I sympathized with her, my heart sank another level because my mom loathed the high-security places like state hospitals, and her mental health never recovered while she was under such extreme stress like that. I shuffled my feet in front of me, with a part of me wishing that someday I could just run away from this drama. Then I tried to lift the mood by saying, "Well, I can't say I wasn't hoping for better news, but I would like to visit her before I head back to Paris. You'll have to give me the info before you drop me off."

"I can do that."

Her casualness about my mom's sickness irritated me, which made me feel strange because I had always wished that my life didn't have to revolve around my mom's mental health. She lacked compassion. I stayed mute the rest of the drive. When she parked the car, I stayed in my seat. I wasn't ready to face the reality of what was going on with my parents. I had gotten used to being in my own bubble in Paris. I didn't have all the emotional drama I always had at home. I had a feeling there was a lot of drama that was about to unravel.

Chapter Three

The stars were starting to peek out from the winter sky by the time Kim and I crossed the parking lot to enter the hospital. Crisp air refreshed my lungs, but I couldn't ignore the fact that I was uneasy. I spent a good deal of my childhood visiting my mom in hospitals, but it was never my dad. I couldn't even remember a time when my dad had been sick with anything more than a routine cold. Sure, it had been a few days since I had talked to him, but he had sounded like his normal self. This sickness had to be some fluke thing that must have hit him all at once. He'd bounce right back out of this place.

A middle-aged woman wearing scrubs greeted us from inside his room. "Are you Abs?"

I shifted my eyes past her, trying to peer inside but she was doing a remarkably good job of blocking me out. I impatiently looked back at her and replied, "I am. How'd you know?"

"I'm Marcie. Your dad's nurse." She finally scooted out of the way, and I entered the room. I was instantly uncomfortable because the surroundings didn't match the scenario that I had prepared myself for. I had expected to see my dad sitting up in a hospital bed, reading something, or perhaps watching something on the wall television. He would definitely smile at me when I peeped my head in the door, and he'd have a funny marketing pitch to explain why he had landed in here. However, this was a little different—actually, completely different. A mellow light glowed from above the bed, but other than that, the room was darkened. My dad was lying on a bed behind a curtain that must have been drawn for privacy.

Marcie shifted her feet, so she was facing me again. "He's been waiting for you." The look she gave me held more sympathy than I was comfortable with. Then she turned to Kim and said, "I'll give you guys some privacy." Pulling the door closed as she walked through it, she left us alone.

I frantically turned to Kim, who was obviously avoiding looking at me, but I pressed anyway. "What's wrong with him?"

She dipped her head toward the curtain. "Why don't you see if he's awake?"

I pulled back the thin curtain, careful to not wake him. I held onto hope that I'd see his boisterous smile perk up when he saw me, but what I saw caused me to startle. His face was too gray to be called pale, and it was sunken in all the places that should exude life. Closed eyes left a peaceful expression on his face, but that was overshadowed by the protrusions of the strong bones in his face showing he was emaciated. It looked like he hadn't eaten in months! *Something wasn't adding up.* I yanked the curtain closed and glared at Kim. In an urgent whisper demanded, "What is going on?"

Her shoulders cringed. "Maybe you can try to wake him. Let him tell you."

"Wake him? He looks dead!" I blurted out, but then I quickly regretted it because as soon as I heard the words, I knew something *was* majorly wrong. "He didn't just collapse because of whatever, right? Something *is* wrong. I can tell."

Her stubborn eyes deferred to my dad.

No matter how hard I pleaded, Kim was determined to remain a closed book. It nudged at my nerves, making me afraid of the secrecy going on. I pulled the curtain back enough for me to slip inside, and as I did, I heard Kim excuse herself out of the room. Now alone with my dad, I padded softly to his bedside and reached out, taking his hand into mine. I briefly closed my eyes out of relief when I felt his hand was warm, even though it was bonier than any hand should ever be. "Dad," I whispered.

His eye lashes fluttered, before opening into shallow slits. I tried to hide my surprise when I saw the dingy yellow of his eyes. "Hi, Dad."

The corners of his mouth bent up when he saw me, but something was different about his gaze. He knew me, but in an unfamiliar way. It felt like he was looking at me from a distance. "Abs, honey." His voice was shallow, lacking oxygen. "I'm glad you came. How are you?"

"Um, confused." The airway in my throat narrowed. Something was wrong—drastically wrong. His eyes looked gigantic next to his deep cheek hallows.

"I'm sorry for the shock," he said apologetically. He took a few breaths like he had run up several flights of stairs. I squeezed his hand, but it had a dual purpose. I partly wanted to comfort him, but I desperately needed to squeeze or pinch something to make sure I wasn't dreaming. He gently squeezed my hand back. I didn't wake up, so I knew this was real life.

I forced a weak grin. "It's okay."

"I've been trying to tell you for months, but you know how I am. I have to find the perfect words, but for the first time in my life, I've found a pitch I can't win." He tried to smile at his joke, but instead he started to cough a deep raspy cough. It took all his strength to ration his breathing through the measured coughs. I found myself holding my breath while I watched him fight the oxygenless waves. When he finally caught a good wind of air, he said, "I've got a touch of pneumonia." He was able to stifle his coughs, but it was evident he was putting all his focus on breathing again.

"Pneumonia?"

With exhausted eyes, he looked back at me and whispered, "And cancer."

My eyebrows tugged upward. I misheard that, and it came out as something really wrong. Leaning in, I focused on his lips to help me hear his weak words. He swallowed before he continued. This time his voice was a little stronger, "I was diagnosed with pancreatic cancer two years ago."

There was that word again: *cancer.* I heard it clearly, but it was like my brain fragmented, immediately resetting to not accept it. Then I focused on the other part of his sentence and really felt lost. "Wait, two years ago?"

He lifted his finger, pointing to his nightstand. My eyes followed his motion, and they landed on a folded sheet of paper. I reached for it and said, "Is this what you want?"

"I've been working on a letter to explain it to you."

I quickly opened the letter. We were past the point of excuses; I needed to know the truth. Before I could scan the first line, I heard my dad urging me to read it out loud.

I don't know how he expected me to read a stupid letter right now but I somehow managed to read it to us both.

Aubergine: I'm so sorry to tell you like this, but I have a secret. When we were living in New York I was diagnosed with pancreatic cancer.

I hesitated. Even while looking at his frail frame, I couldn't believe it. "This can't be true. I would have known." I was desperate for him to tell me this was all some cruel joke. I actually remembered joking about how he must have acquired an illness to make the decision to move to Montana, but I honestly had never seen any clues revealing he was sick. He never responded to my plea, even though I knew he heard me. So, I went back to the letter.

I know you don't know anything about cancer, but pancreatic cancer is one of the worst ones. When I was diagnosed, I was told I would have one year to live.

Again, my eyes alarmedly drew back toward him. This didn't even sound like him. He never spoke in direct comments like that. He always had a pitch for everything. This wasn't pitchy. This was too matter-of-fact. *This was wrong.* "Dad, is this for real?"

His eyes clenched down. "Keep reading."

I took a deep breath, and it came out shaking. I felt like the floor was collapsing beneath me. I read as fast as I could because it was the only way I'd ever be able to read this.

All I could think about was leaving you alone in the world, and I knew I had failed you. You were not ready. I had to fix things, and I didn't have much time to think. I knew you would have no family to rely on since your mother was also in fragile health. I can say this now, because we both know that you have come so far—by the way, I'm so proud of you—but you had a lot to learn back then. Life was so busy in New York, and I knew you would never slow down from school, dance, and friends to learn anything.

My chin was quivering, and I couldn't read anymore. "Dad," I started, "are you saying you lied about Montana?"

He waved his hand to tell me no and he repeated, "Just read." His voice cracked; I about died when it did. This was not my dad! He always had words for *everything*. Not knowing what else to do, I read on.

Eddie and I came up with the plan to move to Montana. It seemed to solve all my problems. I would be able to spend all my time with you and help prepare you for being on your own. Plus, it also solved another problem because the move allowed you to get to know the Rogers'—who love you like a daughter. I hoped and prayed that you would be able to see them as your extended family once I'm gone. They want that too. Please, don't think you will be alone. Eddie and Linda have promised me they will be there for you. They don't want to be invasive with you, though, so the ball is in your court there.

"I don't want them to be my family!" I blurted out. I couldn't believe what he was saying. "I don't need them," I argued. "I have you." When he didn't say anything, I pleaded, "Right, Dad?"

His eyes were closed. He was trying to hide the tears that were spilling his secret as they pooled under his lids. I couldn't watch him suffer like this. This was cruel. He had lied to me, and he couldn't even tell me. "Stop fighting it, Dad," I begged. "Just cry. Just tell me the truth and let it all out." I set the paper down. "I don't want to read this. I want you to tell me what is going on."

"I can't, honey. Just please read it."

"Why, Dad?" I argued. "It's going to tell me that you are dying, and I don't want to read that!" I couldn't believe he would lie to me like this for *two* years! Now, at the last minute he's telling me this. I have no time to prepare.

"I—" he started to respond but broke out into another coughing spell. This one was much worse than the first one. He coughed out air but gagged while he tried to inhale. He was choking. I quickly reached forward to help him sit up straight and instinctively pounded on his back until he gagged. His breath lightened, and he inhaled again. Guilt flooded my heart for being angry. This was not about my feelings. This was something bigger. I dug my teeth into my lip so hard as I found to get my composure. I finally understood what my dad couldn't say out loud. *My dad was leaving me—soon.*

If I cried that it would be unbearable for him, and it was already impossible for him to breathe. Forcing tranquility of mind was something I had mastered in my performance life, and I desperately pulled on this skill to pacify my anguish. My nerves would get so twisted up before a show, and I would force myself into my own alternate reality where I purged out everything but my own body and the stage. I literally would see or hear nothing, and I would feel alone. So, I did that, but the kicker was, I wasn't alone this time. I waited for his breath to slow even more. When I was satisfied that he was no longer choking, I smiled weakly and said, "Don't scare me like that."

He winked at me and pointed to the letter again.

I looked back down at the letter and continued.

But getting back to my diagnosis—with expectations come disappointments and as you remember, your mom wasn't well most of the time we were in Montana. What you didn't know was that my health was failing me fast. Pride is an ugly thing and part of me regrets it now, but I didn't want you to see me get sick. So, I made up that pitch to you about moving back to New York to work for Gabby. You see, I made it seem like it was all about you, but what you didn't know was that it was actually all about me. Gabby took you under her wing as a favor for me. She knew I was dying.

My voice squeaked when I read the word *dying*. I closed my eyes, forcing composure. Again, I wanted to be mad about the lies, but I knew it wasn't about me. When I was ready to continue, I opened my eyes and went back to reading.

As soon as you left for New York, my health declined very quickly, and I didn't want you to see. I wanted you to live your life and learn how to be independent. I didn't want you to feel obligated to stay at the farm to care for me. So, in hindsight, looking back, everything I've put you through these last couple of years wasn't about helping your mom as we let you think, but more about helping you to become the strong independent woman you are. I'm sorry for the dishonesty. It would have killed me sooner if I had to let you see me get sick. I had to stay strong to make sure you were set on a solid path.

I think about how much you have grown. I know your life was hard because of the struggles your mom had, and I used to feel sad about that, but now I see it in a different light. I think it helped you to learn that life isn't always how you want it to be and sometimes you must let it be flawed. I don't want to think about the bad, though. I want you to remember the good times. I've spent a lot of time remembering you when you were little. I remember dancing in the living room with you to I'm a Little Tea Pot. Even with a silly song like that you danced with focus and determination and the most beautiful smile. Then when you started to take ballet, you insisted I learn all the positions as well as you did. I still cry from laughter as I remember falling over my feet when you upgraded my lessons to pirouettes, but you were so determined that I could learn. I never wanted to disappoint you.

The years go so fast. I know that you will do amazing things because you are my Aubergine. I will forever watch over you. St. Augustine used to say, "Learn to dance so when you get to Heaven, the Angels know what to do with you." Well, thanks to you and those early ballet lessons, I have something to do in Heaven, while I wait to dance with my little girl again.

I love you. Dad

My tears fell generously. What he did for me was selfless and beautiful. I had been a total brat these last two years. All he was doing was trying to set me up on a straight path. I set the letter on my lap again and leaned forward and hugged him tightly. "I love you, Dad."

I inhaled his scent deeply, which it told me it wouldn't be long. I let his words trickle slowly through my brain as I pulled up the memories of us dancing in the living room. He was my first dance partner, and the one who had believed in me the most.

I didn't know how to let my dad die. I'm sure it was my instinct, but I did what I always did when I needed to move life through the bad. I took both his hands into mine and I held them. "One last dance, Dad." I moved his hands back and forth gently—the slightest little movement to not wear him—as I pretended to lead him in a dance. A tiny smile laced his lips, and it melted my heart because I knew this was real—this was our final dance. His breath relaxed as I held his hands.

Stricken with guilt, I clearly remembered what a snot I had been in Montana—okay, actually my whole life. I desperately wanted him to brighten up and give me a metaphor that would make this moment better. I scolded myself for all the times I rolled my eyes at him when he would effortlessly try to smooth everything over with his words. I wanted to hear him be happy again. But his words never came.

I thought about his letter and how he said he had wanted to spend his last days with me and that stung the most because *I never knew.* He had a warning. He had a chance to change. I didn't. I never had a chance to change how I treated him. I wouldn't have been so mean. I would've cared more. It wasn't fair that he did all this stuff without telling me. Because I should have been allowed to change too. *I would have loved him better!*

I stayed by his side long into the wee hours of the morning. My adrenaline surged when his breath weakened to new lows. Pulling his hands against my heart, tears erupted from my eyes, and I cried out, "I'm sorry, Dad." I couldn't look at his face because his special essence was gone. His spirit was preparing to leave. Had he been coherent, I would have gone on about how much I appreciated him and how much I needed him. Although I believed that he heard me, I knew he was letting go. There was a weakness that was seeping through his body. I felt it through his hand. When I had the courage to peek at his face again, the skin by his eyes had shallowed out even more. There was a beauty in the moment that I could never describe.

I swear I felt a warmness come down from the heavens, covering the room. Then I was surprised by a tiny smile that grew on his face. Maybe it wasn't a smile. I'm sure someone smarter than me would say it was something technical like gravity pulling his lips—but I told myself that it was a smile, and it was for me, the confirmation that he heard my apology, and it was okay. We did the best we could with what we had. I wanted to hear him call me Aubergine, the name I hated but he had meticulously picked out for me and was so proud of. It was over. Verbal communication was no longer an option, and my heart felt completely devoured in the silence.

Then, like the warmness had come, now it was gone. I was left alone with a stillness, and I knew my dad's spirit was gone. I whispered, "Bye, Dad." My tears fell harder, and my shoulders bent forward in grief as I thought about all the times my dad was there for me. He had never been a perfect dad, but he was loyal to his family. For his loyalty, I would always remember and love him.

Chapter Four

There was a lingering moment that I vaguely remember where the air was quiet before my dad's room was overtaken with professionals. I mostly hugged the wall, observing the rhythm of their work until the scene changed again. In the next scene I was alone, fumbling down the corridor.

Soon after that I found myself entering my parents' condo with the set of keys that had been my dad's. I flicked the light on, and my eyes surveyed the living room filled with all the boring middle-aged people décor. I was unaffected until I noticed the fireplace mantel. My heart felt like a near-miss head-on collision as I eyed my dad's Yankees memorabilia so proudly on display. I let one foot slide forward, and the next one followed until I was standing next to the fireplace.

Then I picked up a glove that he had won at a charity auction. Protective over the autographs, my dad had forbidden me to touch them because he warned the oils from my hand would smear the names. I pushed my hand through the opening in the glove and flexed my fingers to fit, but it was several sizes too big for me. I had never been a fan, but I took time to read each signature, reflecting on how proud this glove had made my dad. Then I slipped off the mitt and put it back on the mantel. It all seemed so silly how he had loved this mitt so much. Now I was here with the stupid mitt and he . . . wasn't.

I was emotionally neutral when I turned on my heel, heading upstairs. The first room on the top of the step was clearly the master bedroom because it was filled with my parents' things. I continued down the hall and peeked into the only other bedroom. The room was small and empty—without even a bed. I hadn't been expecting anything fancy but this was supposed to be *my room* when I came to visit. The reality that there wasn't even a bed set up for me was more than a little jarring.

My dad had booked my plane ticket months ago. The fact that he hadn't prepared a place for me to sleep revealed he had been sick for a while. My guilt crept up my throat because I hadn't visited since I moved overseas. Was it my fault that he never had the chance to tell me he had been sick? After all, I had barely made time to call. I shut the door to the empty guest room and muttered, "This hurts." Then I turned to head back down the stairs and added, "In so many ways."

Now, claiming a spot on the couch, I tried to relax, letting my eyes close. I don't remember sleeping. If I did, it wasn't a restful sleep. I mostly checked the time until I had convinced myself it wasn't too early to call Fulton.

"Happy Thanksgiving." I could hear the smile on his face.

"What? Oh yeah, you too," I replied, having totally forgotten it was a holiday.

"Did you make it in all right?"

"Yeah."

"Are you at your parents' house?"

"Yeah."

"How is it?"

I wondered why my monotone voice hadn't tipped him as being peculiar. I wanted to confide in him, but I had no idea where to start since I didn't know where this story started. When I didn't reply to his question, he asked, "Is everything okay?"

"Not really."

"What's wrong?"

"So, this is going to sound unreal, but when I got here last night, my aunt Kim met me at the airport. She took me to the hospital because my dad had been admitted for pneumonia." I paused, trying to fight through the tightening in my esophagus. "Basically, he was already dying."

"Okay." His voice was so soft it was barely audible.

My eyebrows knitted together. "Okay?"

"I mean, that's crazy. What do you mean dying?"

"When I arrived, he was sick, and I watched him take his final breath last night." My voice stumbled, but I managed to get the words out in one whole statement.

"He passed last night?"

"Yeah."

"Wow, that's terrible. I'm sorry to hear that, but I'm glad you got to be there."

My lips pursed, alerting my what's-going-on sense. There wasn't a lack of empathy in his tone, but it was his word choice that didn't match the situation. He was completely missing the shock factor that was needed. "Don't you want to know why he died?"

"Yeah, of course." His words fumbled out. "What happened?"

"He had cancer for a long time. Since before we were in Montana."

"Really?"

"Yes, Fulton, really." I then waited in silence. Fulton's reaction thus far was odd, even for him. He was normally the furthest thing from a dramatic person, but he had always been extremely sensitive to other people's pain.

"Okay, I'll admit it," Fulton blurted out, then continued before I had a chance to ask him what he was guilty of. "I'm having a hard time with this conversation, and I don't know what to say because I feel terrible you had to walk into that, and you just lost your dad, but you keep asking me these questions and I can't lie. . ."

Lie. I hadn't known Fulton had anything to lie about. This conversation was taking an entirely different course than it should be. I held my chest and asked, "What can't you lie about?"

"I knew your dad was dying."

His words rang in my ear and then repeated and echoed. An atomic bomb could have gone off in the room. I wouldn't have heard it, because I was hyper-tuned into his words. "What do you mean you knew? I didn't even know."

"It's sort of one of those things that got messy." His words were spaced out so far, they lost their cohesion. Then he added, "I hated that I knew."

My heart crescendoed, sending a wave of nausea that crashed into my gut. Fulton was confessing a real *lie.* I triple blinked. "Wait. What did you know?" I needed clarification.

"I knew he was dying," Fulton repeated. His breathing on the other side of the phone reassured me that he hadn't bolted from our conversation, but his pause hinted this discussion was going to be hard. Then he continued, "And that's why I encouraged you to visit now."

"How did you know that?" I asked, but a sickening feeling dug further into my gut, taunting me that I already knew the answer.

"You know, your dad always told my parents all that stuff." His voice was careful, but I could hear an uneasiness as well. "And sometimes my parents shared it with me."

"What stuff? What do you mean always?" I set my jaw forward, waiting to understand.

"Oh wow." Fulton breathed heavily into the phone. "This's tough to talk about. I wish I was there. I had no idea I'd have to explain this over the phone."

"Explain what over the phone?" I pressed. I wasn't naïve to my parents' deception. Over the years, there had been many things they had failed to tell me, citing it was for my protection. I always heard the rumors and honestly ignored it because I was usually better off not knowing everything, but even with all the mistruths of the past, I had never been completely in the dark about something so huge. By now I had pieced together that this wasn't about *one* lie anymore. This was an epic soap opera pile of lies that at this point I didn't even care to understand, at least not from my parents' perspective. I was used to it. However, I did care that this was Fulton. Fulton didn't lie to me. This was changing things.

"Okay. I'll tell you from the start," he finally said.

I don't know why I felt like I was in the middle of an emergency. My dad had already died. My trauma should have been over, but the last thing I would have expected was for Fulton to know something about my life that I didn't. Fulton was never the kind of guy to keep a secret from me. He had to be the most honest person I had ever met.

"I knew your dad was sick before we even moved to Montana."

"What! How—"

He cut me off. "I was told *not to tell you,* and it wasn't my secret to tell. However, I knew that's why we left the city."

The only other time I felt anything close to this was when I had slipped a landing on a leap in my second year of ballet. I fell forward and took Erica's knee right into my gut. But as bad as that hurt, this pain was still worse—this was a betrayal. "How could you lie to me?"

"I wasn't lying."

"No? Well, you didn't tell me the truth, so how is that not a lie?"

"I admit it was a form of dishonesty. I had a hard time with it, but it wasn't my lie. I remember being at dinner with you when your parents told you we were moving, and they said it was for all these weird reasons. I couldn't even look at you. I couldn't keep their lie going if I looked at you."

"You knew back then!" I exclaimed. I got off the couch. If I didn't move, I would explode or something. "I remember that dinner. I thought you avoided me because you were upset about the move too."

"I was upset about the move, but I was furious that everyone was lying to you by refusing to tell you about your dad. I knew it was wrong. I thought about how I would feel if my dad was dying, and no one was honest with me. It would have crushed me."

"Did everyone know?"

After a short pause, he confirmed, "Everyone but you."

"You have got to be kidding."

"I wish I was, but it's been excruciatingly difficult to keep quiet about this the whole time. I remember one time I almost told you."

"When?" I didn't waste words questioning him. I couldn't remember him saying anything close to my dad is dying in Montana.

"Do you remember when I got mad at you that first day when we went out to pick berries and you were being mean to your parents? I was annoyed that they were lying to you, but I knew you wouldn't have been so harsh to them if you had known the truth. I desperately wanted to tell you to be nice to your dad, but I knew that would be suspicious to tell you that. I tried to cover it up by saying you were mean to everyone."

"That's why you told me to stop being mean! I thought it was because you didn't want to have to put up with me." My mind raced through all the things my family and the Rogers' had said to me over the last couple of years. Did everything have a double meaning? I felt so cheated, so lied to, so exploited. "So, basically you guys all thought I was too dumb to care?"

"No, I didn't think that. I knew you would care. I knew it would kill you. I wanted you to know, but it wasn't *my* secret to tell."

"So, you lied to me for two years."

"No."

"No, you didn't lie? Because I don't think you told me the truth."

"It wasn't like that. It wasn't my secret to tell," he repeated and then added, "I'm sorry you must hear about this from me, but I had to be honest. It felt wrong to listen to you talk about your dad's passing and to act surprised."

"Oh, right. Now you must be honest. Because it was easy now, but you couldn't be honest before?"

"It wasn't easy. I knew that if your dad finally told you about his secret that I didn't need to honor it anymore. I hated it. Trust me. I hated every bit of it."

There was a lingering sting in my heart that told me that everything he said was true, but it was also changing things for us. I literally felt like my whole life had been exposed as a fraud. That was bad enough, but to think about Fulton knowing and not telling me was more than I could handle. "I'm disappointed in you. I thought you were better than that."

"That's not fair."

"You want to know what I don't think is fair? You lying to me for years about my dad being sick. I thought the whole point of a relationship is to be honest."

"We weren't dating when I found this out, and it wasn't something I could blurt out when we started dating. How would I even bring it up?"

"I don't know but I sort of feel like things change when you are dating someone, and any secret needs to be brought out into the open. Do you have any other secrets you are keeping from me? I suppose next you are going to tell me all about my mom and what happened to her and why she is in the nut house again?"

Fulton's silence said it all.

"You know about my mom too?" I held my chest as I couldn't take the building pressure anymore. "I can't believe this. How can you be such a liar?"

"It's not my fault your parents talk to my parents!"

"No, but it is your fault you keep secrets from me! That's not okay. We are in a relationship, and secrets shouldn't be a part of it."

"Your dad always insisted that you be protected from that stuff because he wanted you to focus on building your life so that when he died, you would have options. I'm sorry."

"Me too."

"I understand why you're mad. I wish it was different, but it all got really messy. I got dragged into the middle of it for years before we were even dating—"

I cut him off because it didn't matter what excuses he had for me. I would never be able to see this as anything other than a betrayal. "This is too raw. It's my whole life you lied about." I closed my eyes to focus clearly on my words. "Everything I was living the last few years was a lie, and you knew it."

"It wasn't my lie," he repeated, but this time his voice pitched higher.

"I think it was."

"I cannot have this conversation over the phone. It's too important. I'll come see you—"

"There's no point. I don't feel like there is a need to continue—"

"I think you need to take some time to digest everything that has happened," Fulton cut in. "Then after you have time to grieve, I'll come visit you so we can talk about this."

"What is there to talk about?" I was annoyed at his persistence but then I had a bad thought, and immediately blurted it out, "Or are you hiding more from me?"

"No!" he shouted, but then in almost a whisper he added, "You know everything now."

I could tell by his voice that he was emotional. As mad as I was at him, it totally stunk because Fulton wasn't just my boyfriend and my best friend. He was my everything. The exhaustion from the last twenty-four hours started to flood over me. I decided to give myself some grace and let this go—for now. "Maybe you're right. I need some time to think. I'm going to let you go. I'll get ahold of you before I go back to Paris. Maybe we can meet up to talk."

He let out a huge sigh. "I'll make plans to come to the funeral before I head back to New York. We can talk . . ."

"Yeah. I'm maxed out."

"I understand. I'll let you go. I'm so sorry about your dad and everything . . ."

"I know."

"Talk to you soon?"

"Goodbye," I said quickly and ended the call. I knew hanging up on Fulton would break his heart, but I didn't care. He broke *my* heart. I'm not about revenge or anything like that, but I wasn't able to consider his feelings right now.

I kept replaying all the moments over the years when someone said something and I understood it to mean one thing, but now I second-guessed it, assuming everyone had always lied to me. My brain was so full of fake memories that kept building up more pressure. My head was going to detonate. I needed a valve or something that I could adjust to let out some of the stress. But I didn't have a valve, and I couldn't take it anymore, so I sobbed. It was moments like these that I ached for dance and the beautiful distraction that it had been. I couldn't grieve that part of my life too, so I quickly pushed the urge away. I picked up my phone and scrolled through videos for an emergency distraction, finally settling on a new version of The Sleeping Beauty Ballet. I clicked on it and zoned out, begging my emotions to numb. I was gutted and unable to deal with reality, so I cried for hours until I finally was able to zombie out on the couch to binge even more tragic ballets on the internet. All while I ignored the fact that everything was broken.

Chapter Five

I slept through most of the weekend, not wanting to be awake. When the Monday morning air wafted under my nose, had I not known better I would have detected it to held a spring scent. I grumbled at the sweet smell and rolled over. I would have selected the weather to be hammering rain, or a typical November snow blizzard, or heck, even a hurricane—something horrible to match my mood. As my luck would have it, it was unusually warm for this time of year. In addition to my undesired sun rays, I was saluted by birds chirping outside the living room window. I rolled over on the couch, grabbed a pillow, and smothered it over my ear.

After only a moment, I gave up trying to sleep and picked up my phone and scrolled through my messages while I walked to the bathroom. A text from Fulton rested on my home screen but I stubbornly refused to read it. I tried to ignore the eerie absence of my almost daily texts from my dad. I already missed him so much.

This was going to take some time.

While I washed up, I thought about my mom, wondering if I should call ahead to see what kind of mood she was in before I visited her. I quickly tossed that idea down the toilet because I knew she would be in a terrible mood. What choice did I have? She was my mother, and her husband had just died. She had a right to know. I did what any good daughter would do. I took a cab to Kim's house, so we could tell her together—safety in numbers.

When I arrived at Kim's house, she was tidying up the kitchen. "Come on inside and take a seat while I get the dishwasher loaded," she called from the top of her steps. I let myself in and did my best to step over the piles of mismatched shoes and sweatshirts that littered the stairs while I followed her voice. "I have four kids, and I just put them on the bus. If I don't do cleanup now, I won't ever get it done, because by the time we get back, they'll be back off the bus. Then my work starts all over again."

I helped myself to a seat at the kitchen island. I only remembered meeting her one other time in my life—at my grandma's funeral—but she seemed welcoming and normal enough to talk to, so I struck up a conversation. "Thanks for agreeing to go with me on such short notice."

"Oh, you're welcome." She stacked plates in the dishwasher while she talked. "I'm glad you asked. I feel like I need to be more present in Claire's life, but she makes it incredibly agonizing, so I chicken out. I don't know. I have always felt inadequate when it comes to her." She looked up at me, and her face was pinched. "And like a failure."

"You too?" I replied, adding in my sarcastic tone. "She has a way of making everyone in her path feel terrible about themselves. She can't ever be happy."

"I'm not sure it's something she knows how to do." Kim rinsed off the silverware under the running water and then started placing them in the silverware basket. "I tried for years to be there, but after a while and especially after I had kids, I had to decide that I couldn't heal her. I couldn't ruin my own life—and my kids' life. It was heartbreaking to come to that conclusion, but I had to for my own family's sake."

Her words hit me in all the ways I needed to be woken up. She said all the things that I could have said about my mom but never had the strong voice to do it. From the few minutes of conversation that I had with Kim, she seemed fairly normal. Maybe that's why my mom hated her? She was jealous. Feeling overwhelmed, I asked, "Do you know why she is the way she is?"

She stopped and turned toward me. "You don't?"

I raised my eyebrows. "You do?"

Her eyes brushed thoughtfully over my face with an expression I could only describe as maternal. "Come with me. I'll show you something."

I followed her upstairs and into her bedroom where she went to the closet, reached to the bottom, and retrieved a small wooden chest, like something for keepsakes. When she opened it, pictures that were stuffed to the top started to slip and fall onto the ground. She did her best to gather while at the same time sorting them into different piles. She seemed to know an order to the disorganization, and she dug right to a chunk of pictures at the bottom. While she straightened out the small pile of pictures, she started to explain. "I'm guessing no one ever told you this. It's sort of the family secret."

"If it's a secret, then why are you telling me?" I spoke cautiously because I had my fill of family secrets this week. I wasn't sure if I could handle another one.

Taking a seat on the bed, she motioned for me to sit next to her, and I did. "I don't like to dance around stuff. I'm a straight shooter. Plus, I've learned family secrets have different perspectives. I've come to terms with this one better than everyone else. It hasn't been easy. It's not pretty. It's sad. But I don't have a problem talking about it." She flipped through the pictures until she found the one that she wanted, holding it out for me to see. "Do you know anything at all about Claire's childhood?"

I thought about the things my mom had told me over the years. She had mentioned how they grew up in poverty, never had enough, and there was a lot of arguing. I didn't know anything specific. "Not really," I admitted.

"I can start at the beginning." She pointed to the picture displaying a man, a woman and three little girls lined up in front of them. "This was our mom and dad, both of whom were immigrants when they came here. My dad worked as a plumber's helper, and my mom did different things to try to earn money but mostly stayed home. She never learned English. She was smart—actually extremely well-read in Italian—but she didn't have the confidence to learn a new language, and as you can imagine the inability to communicate created many issues while you are trying to raise a family."

"I would think so," I agreed.

She pointed to the girls in the photo. "Here we are, us girls. I'm the oldest. Never mind my weird bangs. It was the style back then to have bangs take up half your head." She snickered and then moved her finger over to the next tallest girl. "This is Claire. I think she was about five or so in this picture."

I leaned over, taking in the simplicity of my mom's smile and plain dress. I could feel Kim watching me study the picture, making me uncomfortable. I don't know why, but I would have loved to look at this picture in private. Since she was waiting for me, I quickly looked back at her. "It looks like her."

"This was about a week before it happened. Then everything changed . . ."

"What happened?"

She pointed to the smallest girl in the photo. "Do you know about Liz?"

"No." I assumed it was a sister because she was lined up in a family photo, but I had never heard that name before. "What about her?"

"So, Liz was our youngest sister—a real doll. She was sweet and silly, kind and everything you could want in a sister. And she was Claire's best friend. They were only three years apart, and they were obsessed with each other."

"She looks like a real sweety." I looked down at her chubby cheeks and slightly bushy eyebrows that matched my mom's. Then I paused, stuck on her eyes, which were almond- shaped and deep-set like mine. Her nose was upturned like mine too. There was something familiar about how she smiled back at the camera—she had my smile. "She looks a little like me," I said thoughtfully.

Kim bowed her head further over the picture. "She looks exactly like you."

"I see it too," I agreed, "but how come I've never met her?"

"As I was saying, your mom and she were best friends, and they did everything together. One year, one of them got sick with something. I'm not sure who got it first, but it always happened that when one of them got a cold or a virus, the other one would get it right away too. They each had a high fever that scared my mom. After a couple of days where the fever didn't go down, my mom took them both to the doctor. The doctor wrote down instructions for my mom on how to care for them. This is when it got sad." She stopped, latching her eyes with mine.

I lifted my eyebrows, acknowledging that I was listening. Then she continued, "My mom was a good mom. But like I said, she didn't speak English well, and she read even less of it. She didn't understand the instructions the doctor had given to her, and when she tried to read them, it only made things worse because she got it mixed up. The virus was a normal virus. The fever was a normal fever, and it should have been treated like any other. The doctor wrote on the list to make sure the girls got lots of water and fluids, but my mom had read it wrong. She read that the girls were to get *no* water or fluid."

My lips turned down as I thought about how wrong that sounded. Everyone knows that you need to stay hydrated when you are sick, I thought. "Why would you avoid water?"

"Well, you don't, but she was trying hard to do what the doctor said, so when she got home, she told the girls they couldn't have any water until after their fevers were gone."

"Didn't they get thirsty or crabby?"

Kim rubbed the back of her neck. "I don't remember it well because I was in school, but I do know that my mom was scared because they were so sick. She wanted desperately for them to get better. She was strict about not giving them any water, but your mom, Claire, wasn't ever a rule follower. She wasn't scared of getting into trouble. She snuck into the bathroom and took sips of water out of the faucet when my mom wasn't paying attention. Lizzy was thirsty too, but she was too little to get her own water as she was only two. Your mom confessed to me once that Lizzy begged her to get some water too, but your mom didn't want to get Lizzy in trouble. So, after about a day with those high fevers and no water, Lizzy started to appear sleepy. My mom thought she was resting because of the fever. After she didn't make a noise for a while, they realized she was unresponsive. By the time they were able to get her to the doctor and explain what happened, it was too late."

"She died?" My heart wrenched for the little girl I had never even heard of. "How awful."

"It didn't take long for my mom to blame Claire."

"How?" I interrupted.

"You see, Claire was drinking water that whole time, so she was getting better. When my mom saw her improvement, that confirmed for her that the no-fluid protocol was working. She didn't know Claire was lying about the water. My mom had no idea what was really going on."

"So, your mom blamed my mom for Lizzy's death?"

"I think so." She smoothed her hair back, tucking it back behind her ear then said, "But I know that Claire blamed herself too. Aside from missing her best friend and blaming herself, everything changed after that. Our family sort of lost its bond. Nobody wanted to talk about Lizzy because we all missed her. We all felt responsible and like we should have known better."

"But you didn't know," I said, feeling defensive because the whole situation seemed so unfortunate.

She shrugged her shoulders. "I knew how to read English better than my mom. I have always wished I would have tried to read the note too. Maybe I could have caught the error. There was a lot of blame over the years. Then our family didn't function anymore, and we fought a lot. We blamed each other for everything all the time. Now that I look back on it, I think what we really wanted to do was blame each other for Lizzy's death. We could never say her name."

I don't think I've never had more clarity about my mom as I did in that moment. "So that's why my mom is crazy?"

"I think it's part of it."

"What's the rest of it?" I was scared to ask.

She looked back down at the photo and pointed to Liz. "Your mom was okay at pretending she was fine until she had you."

"Me? What did I do?"

She tapped the picture with her finger, touching Lizzy. "You look exactly like her."

My jaw fell open as I now understood why my mom hated me. Why she couldn't love me. Why she was never able to be there for me. Everything that I had struggled with my whole life, everything that I thought was my fault—it made sense now. My gut had always told me I was the one to make her crazy, but I didn't understand what I could have possibly done wrong. *I understood.* I didn't do anything. I made my mom crazy because I looked like her dead sister who she blamed herself for killing. I finally understood.

Chapter Six

I'm astonished my dad hadn't created a metaphor for how it felt to be a somewhat sane person arriving at a mental hospital. All the normal adjectives that people use to describe situations never applied well to this. The nearest example I could muster up would be like leaving the Matrix for an alternate reality. Things had a different rhythm in these places.

By now, I had time to contemplate what I had learned about my mom's sister, but a few things still bothered me. I wanted to understand before I had to face my mom. While we walked through the corridors in search of my mom's room, I attempted to clarify my thoughts with Kim. "I'm having a hard time thinking about my mom and Liz. Have you ever tried to talk about it with her?"

"Nah, my whole family sort of buried the incident with her."

"Did my dad know?"

She shrugged her shoulders. "I don't know. I knew better than to bring it up."

"Do you think that's why she didn't get along with you? Did you remind her of Liz?"

She inclined her head before relenting. "I think that was part of it."

"Boy, it's crazy how one little piece of information changes everything. I'm seeing her so differently. It's definitely been a clearwater moment for me."

Kim reached out, touching my forearm. "I never knew how much you struggled with things with your mom. Please don't blame yourself."

I spotted my mom's room number, and we froze in the hall, waiting to finish our talk. I asked in a low voice, "How come you never told me earlier?"

She whispered, "Your mom didn't let me talk to you much. Like I said, she didn't like me, and I knew it would only cause a bunch of stress for her if I forced myself into your life and brought up a bunch of old stuff. I had to let it go at the time. Besides, there wasn't anything you could do. It's not like you could change your face."

I lowered my eyes, feeling them start to cloud with memories. I couldn't help but think about a couple of the small moments in my childhood that had been confusing at the time but now seemed nuanced. There was one time in particular that came to mind, which was when I had been playing in the sand at the beach. I must have been barely in grade school, and I hadn't learned to swim yet. I wasn't allowed near the water that day because the tide was coming in strong, but I wanted to get a bucket of water for my sandcastle. So, I snuck up to the water's edge while my mom lay on her beach towel to relax. Then I quickly filled my bucket and turned to run back, but I froze when I noticed she had sat up with her eyes fixated on me. My eyes raced to confirm her fuzzy unibrow, but instead she was gazing at me with uncharacteristically warm eyes. It startled me because she didn't usually spend much time looking at me, except for a quick supervisory glance to make sure I wasn't getting into trouble. I waited for her to scold me, but she never did. She stayed mute the whole time I tip-toed back to my sand pile with my bucket. If I hadn't known better, I would have sworn I had seen love in her eyes. It was a moment that I held onto in the bad times when she would become unbraided. It was that expression that made me have hope even in the lowest moments.

Kim knocked on the door, and my mind recoiled back to the present. We didn't have to wait long before we heard her call, "Come in." I shuffled my feet a few times before I forced them to move forward into the room. My mom sat up in her bed with her eyes glued to a magazine in her lap. Her hair was tied back in a low ponytail like she always wore it, and even though she looked good for her age with her makeup-free face, she had aged since the last time I had seen her with even more cracks on the corners of her eyes.

"Hi, Mom," I meekly greeted her, holding my breath, waiting for her to notice me. Her eyes landed on mine for the briefest of moments before they bounced over to acknowledge Kim. "I figured you left me here to rot."

She held a sly twist on her lips, so I couldn't tell what sort of mood she was in. I instinctively side-stepped so I was out of her direct line of vision. While I was dodging, Kim stood her ground and simply said, "Claire, I'm not going to spend time with you if you are mean to me. You need to decide if you want to see us or not. If you are going to be rude, we are leaving."

My mom squared her shoulders, and I expected a rapid-fire reply, but her voice softened when she said, "No, you can come in."

My eyes bolted back to Kim, and I marveled at the way she had reeled my mom in. My dad never did that, nor did he allow me to say anything like that to her. In fact, I had often wondered what her response would have been if we had stopped tiptoeing around her moods. Kim took a few steps into the room and rested her back against the wall. "So, we came here today to tell you some bad news."

My mom's face faded to a tell-tale shade of white. "It's Cole."

Kim didn't waste any words and said, "Yes."

My mom's eyes drifted down until they were completely shut, and she asked, "When?"

"Two days ago," Kim said. This time her voice held an air of empathy, but it was still more matter-of-fact than I could have ever managed.

"I knew it was close because he had stopped calling."

"Abs was there. She said he was peaceful."

I waited for my mom to open her eyes and turn to me, asking me how he had been, or how I was, or how I felt about the family secret of my dad's cancer finally being out in the open. I wanted her to apologize for not telling me the truth about my dad and for lying to me about why we had moved. I wanted her to tell me it was okay to grieve for my dad, that she knew he had been proud of me, and that I would be fine without him. I moistened my lips, waiting but she didn't do any of that. She simply tucked her chin down further and said, "Thanks for telling me." Oddly, the sting I should have felt was numbed because of my new clarity. I finally understood that she *couldn't* open her eyes because she would *see* me and seeing me is what bothered her *the most*. I had spent my life wanting to understand, but now that I understood, it wasn't enough. I still *needed* her.

I should have left the room, like any sane person would have. After years of being rejected, I knew better. Instead, my feet awkwardly gravitated forward until I was by her bed. Even after dropping to my knees, I could feel my legs shake. I lifted my chin and pleaded, "Can we do this together, Mom?" I imagined her being a small child, having to watch her sister die, and feeling the blame for it. I figured she had some of those same feelings of loss creep up again, and it had to be unbearable. I wanted to be strong for her. I started to ramble, "I'm hurting too, Mom. You don't have to shut down like you always do. It makes me feel like my emotions are wrong, and they aren't. I had to watch Dad die. I need to do this with you. Can we grieve together?"

Her eyes remained clenched, and I instantly regretted my moment of vulnerability. My empathy was quickly replaced with anger, and I fought back every urge I had to physically take my fingers and force her to open her stupid eyelids. "Look at me, Mom," I begged. Her stubborn shoulders stiffened but that was all that changed.

I rolled my head back and looked at the ceiling. *I was so not surprised.* I didn't even feel hurt anymore. Out of the corner of my eyes, I could see Kim extend her hand out to me like she was reaching for one of her smaller children. "Come on, Abs. Let's give her some space."

My legs were heavy when I tried to stand again. I had dreaded coming here because I had no idea what I would say to her. Now that I was here, I felt this pull toward her. Even after she rejected me, I yearned to be accepted. It made me want to scream at her that she wasn't the only one hurting. It was pointless. Her mental stuff was so deep-rooted that I doubted she'd ever heal.

I somberly followed Kim out the door, knowing I wouldn't try to visit her again. I saw very clearly that my dad had been the glue. My mom had never wanted anything to do with me. I understood why my dad had been desperate for me to create a life of my own last year. At least now I was used to taking care of myself. My dad had known all along that this was what would happen, and he had prepared me for it. For that, I was grateful.

Chapter Seven

Back in the car, I was newly energized with the need to further my and Kim's conversation about my mom's childhood. But it was more than that: I was drawn to Kim because she had a non-apologetic strength that I had quickly learned to admire. I knew that if I wanted to get past the hurt that I carried around with me over the way my mom had treated me, I would have to learn to be more like Kim. I waited until she was back on the interstate before I brought it up. "I was thinking about something."

"What's that?"

"Well, whenever my mom would have an episode where she would lose herself and go into her fits, she would run away . . ." I chewed my lip while I strung together the memories, but it made so much sense now. I had to get it off my chest. "We would find her by water. Water was a comfort for her, but now I wonder if the water was more of a symbol of Liz and what happened."

Kim gave no facial clues to her emotions. She truly was one of those people who had learned to not mix her emotions with facts, and I was mesmerized by the control she had over herself. She finally said, "It could be. Most of the stuff Claire does is hard to understand. Was she happier next to water?"

"I don't know if I could tell either way. It had always seemed like she enjoyed watching the water because she would zone out like nothing else existed."

"It would be nice to know what she was thinking." She glanced at me and then said, "Wouldn't it?"

"It would make it a lot easier."

We fell into a melancholy silence for the rest of the trip. When we got to my street, she turned to me and said, "I guess we can assume your mom is not coming to your dad's funeral."

"Nope, I don't suppose we can rely on her for that." I stared at my feet. I can't believe I still had to go through the process of burying my dad by *myself*. Wait, I didn't necessarily have to do it by myself. I lifted my gaze back to her. "Are you coming?"

"Well, yeah." The was an air in her voice that said she wouldn't have it any other way. "I'll be there for you."

Her pulled into my driveway, and I had an overwhelming peace flow through me. *She was going to be there for me.* Not only at the funeral but after that too. I didn't even know this woman, but I felt it. She was strong and honest. She shifted her car into park and said, "My kids get off the bus at four. I need to head back right away, but you can call me if you need anything."

I unclicked my seatbelt and was about to say goodbye, but I had a gnawing in my brain. It wasn't going to leave me unless I brought it up. I turned back. "Do you think my mom kept you away from me on purpose?"

Kim tipped her chin up, leveling her gaze with mine. "How so?"

"She always told me how terrible you were and how I wouldn't like you. What do you think the lies were all about?"

She offered yet another shrug. "Again, I'm not going to pretend to know what she was thinking."

"Did you think it was weird when my parents moved here?"

"I did think it was weird, until I learned it wasn't your mom's decision. It was your dad's. I think he knew your mom would need *someone* to watch over her, and you would too."

"Did my dad ask you to watch over me?"

She shook her head so softly that if my eyes wouldn't have been glued to her, I would not have noticed any movement at all. "He didn't have to."

When I didn't say anything, she added, "I'm a mom. I know." Her words were so honest and unexpected that they acted like a healing balm on the wounds that my mom had cratered into my heart. I had never expected her. "I'd better let you get home," I said, starting to feel bad for lingering after she told me she needed to leave. "I'll see you Thursday for the funeral."

She winked at me. "You bet."

I got out of the car, and I was oddly at peace. If I hadn't known better, I would have sworn my dad's hand was in all of this. I felt him nudge me closer to Kim while at the same time it was like I was being given an allowance to be strong and let my mom go. It was hard to describe as anything other than a quieting. *It was from my dad.* As I let myself into the house, I was okay because I knew my dad was still making deals for me—even from up above.

Chapter Eight

That night it dawned on me after I had already shut the lights off for bed that I hadn't called Gabby yet, and she was expecting me to show up to work tomorrow. I grappled for my phone, ignored the multiple unread texts from Fulton and pressed send on Gabby's name.

"Hi, Abs."

"Hey, how are things going?"

"Crazy. I have so much freight that needs to be out on the floor and it's not happening. Black Friday was insane."

"That's good. That means our hard work paid off."

"Yes, it did," she agreed, and then she put me on the spot with a change of subject. "Are you ready for work tomorrow?"

I swallowed, taking enough time that it must have made Gabby suspicious, and she asked, "Are you back yet or were your flights messed up?"

"No, I'm not back. I changed my return flight, and I'm sorry I forgot to tell you. It's been weird . . ."

Her voice slowed. "What do you mean weird?"

I knew from the letter that my dad had written me that Gabby already knew my dad had been sick, but I wasn't sure if she was aware of anything else. I steadied my words as best as I could to avoid crying. "I didn't know before, but my dad told me that he had confided in you about his cancer. When I got here, he was sick, and well, he passed away . . ."

"Already?" There was an awe in her voice that hung low in the air.

"Yeah." I matched her tone in respect, knowing that she had been my dad's friend, so this had to be hard for her to hear as well.

"I'm sorry." She hesitated and then asked, "Did he finally tell you about everything?"

"I don't know." I shook my head to no one, but it was a necessary release of the budding disgust in my chest. "I'm sort of learning about things as I go along," I explained. Then dug deep for courage and asked, "What did you know?"

"It doesn't matter what I knew," she said, gently brushing my inquiry away. "I'm sorry to hear about his passing. I know this has to be devastating for you."

"It's hard but it's not." My honesty brought a small release of tension in my chest that begged me to continue to speak—not to appease her question but because I needed to hear more of my own honest feelings. "In a way, there's a clarity to a lot of what has happened over the last two years. I thought everything was too extreme and not fair, but now a lot of things that my dad said or did make sense. So, in a weird way, that part feels better for me. But losing him is weird. I don't think I've really processed it yet especially since I normally didn't see him much anyway." Gabby and I had worked closely for the last two years. Since the only thing the two of us did was work, we were sort of best friends. I trusted her, and I was ready to hear more so I pressed, "Can you tell me what you knew? I won't be mad. Please."

"Ah," she said. That was what she did when she was overwhelmed. I waited with trust, and then she finally said, "I knew when Cole left New York that he was sick. He said the doctors gave him a year, but he was trying to change everything. Part of me thought he was in denial. I wondered if he thought the cancer would disappear if he ignored it, but I didn't judge him for taking a drastic approach. And . . . I knew things weren't going well when he sent you to New York that week when I met you. I knew he had that transfusion—"

"Wait," I said, cutting her off. "What transfusion? Didn't he tell you he was helping my mom?"

"No, from what I understood, she was transferred into her new treatment place. I don't remember for sure what was going on—maybe an issue with his blood platelets—but he was in the hospital that whole time you were here. That's why he was so desperate and willing to have you out of state."

I gasped. "What?" Somehow, I managed to speak my words of confusion in a normal tone. "That's a whole different story than the one I had."

"I'm sorry. I know this stinks."

"It stinks in so many ways; I can't even comprehend it. I've been so busy trying to understand everything that I haven't had time to even grieve."

"Oh, you will. Don't worry. When my parents died, I never cried until the funeral—both times. I was so preoccupied with arrangements that I didn't have time to process it. When is the funeral?"

"It's tomorrow. But my dad had made all the plans already with the funeral home, so I had very little to plan. Maybe that's also why everything feels unreal."

"It could be. I'm so sorry. You take as much time as you need to wrap up everything there."

"Thank you for saying that. I was worried about work and how much we have going on. I know this is the worst timing."

"There is never a good time for this type of stuff."

"Right."

"Okay, I can let you go so you can get ready for tomorrow. Do you have anyone to help you through the funeral? Is Fulton coming?"

The mention of his name made the pit in my stomach wrench. "I don't know. I'm guessing because he's Fulton, and he's so reliable that he'll be here, but I've been avoiding his calls."

"Why?" She sounded alarmed.

"I know it's bad, but when I called him, he confessed he already knew about my dad too. It destroyed my heart to hear that he had been lying to me this whole time. So, I actually haven't talked to him since then."

"What do you think not talking is going to do? Do you think you're going to break up with him?"

"I don't know. I feel like I'm being nagged constantly by the fact that he lied to me about my whole life, and I don't understand how I'm ever supposed to trust him now."

"He didn't really lie. He kept the same secret we were all keeping, and it wasn't to ever do anything to betray you. It was a favor to your dad. You don't sound mad at me, and I knew."

"That's different. You were my dad's friend first. And maybe I'm not surprised now since I've been through so much these last couple of days. But with Fulton, I trusted that he was different. He was my evergreen."

"I'm going to be honest with you, Abs, I don't think you should break up with him. I think you let him know that you are hurting but this situation clearly wasn't his fault. He was caught in the middle."

"That's easy for you to say. How do I trust him?"

"You trust him because he's Fulton. Come on, you know he's easily the best thing to happen to you. This mess wasn't his. So maybe his flaw is that he was being loyal to your dad to a fault, but I don't see that as a bad thing. I bet he is relieved to finally have it out in the open."

"I still feel betrayed," I whispered, because the words were getting hard to say.

"I know. But you are placing the blame on the wrong person. I think you need to think about it and at least try to move past it. Give him another chance. Trust me. He is worth it. Guys like him don't come around every day."

On one hand, I knew she was right. Fulton was amazing, and my gut told me that he was trustworthy, but my heart was still deeply wounded. "I don't know. Maybe I'll talk to him and see how it goes."

"There you go. That's exactly what you need to do. Relationships are work. This is not going to be the last hiccup you have."

"How'd you get so smart about this stuff?" I asked with a suspicious tone.

"I used to watch soap operas with my grandma when I was little. Trust me, it gets worse than this," she said with more sincerity than sarcasm.

"Okay," I slowly agreed. "I'll take your advice and talk to him. And I'll text you when I know what day I can come back to work."

"Deal."

"Thank you for listening to my issues," I said.

"You're welcome. Take care and see you soon."

I ended the call, and I was about to set my phone down but convinced myself I had a text to send.

Me: *Fulton, sorry I've been MIA. It's been a hard week. Let me know when you get to town. I want to talk before the funeral if possible.*

I hit send and then stared at my phone, waiting for his reply. To my surprise, he didn't text me back. The silence was unnerving because Fulton wasn't a guy to play games or even avoid confrontation. Something was up with him now.

Chapter Nine

That night instead of going to bed, I zoned out watching the
Romeo and Juliet ballet death scene on repeat for hours. I wanted
to cry but unfortunately my eyes stayed dry no matter what tragedy
I forced myself to watch. Somewhere in the wee hours of the
morning, I must have nodded off, but I didn't sleep long before
my anxiety caused me to wake in an unfounded panic.

I instinctively grabbed for my phone, expecting a text from
Fulton but still nothing. My heart jerked back when I realized he
might be mad at me for blowing him off. I thought about texting
him again, but he had gotten my first text. If he wanted to talk
to me, he would. Avoidance was so different for us. We had never
fought before. I wanted to call him, but instead texted Kim. I
pleaded with her to come over before the funeral. There was no
way I could arrive alone.

Then I halfheartedly dragged my feet upstairs to get dressed for
the funeral. I didn't even have to look in my dance bag to know
I hadn't packed anything appropriate to wear. I let out a deep
breath. I needed to borrow something from my mom. How crazy

is that? I never borrowed her clothes ever when we lived together. I tucked my bottom lip in and slowly opened her bedroom door. Then I beelined to my mom's closet, careful to not let my eyes draw to my dad's clothes hanging in the same closet. With laser focus, I filed through my mom's dresses until I came upon a plain black midi dress. She was a couple sizes bigger than I was, but I could make it work. I found a chunky belt to cinch the waist and left the room without touching anything else.

I was brushing my eyebrows when my phone rang. My heart knew it was Fulton, and I accepted his video call and sat down to focus.

"Hey you," I replied. "I wasn't expecting you to call."

"I figured that."

He was wearing my favorite t-shirt. It was a light hazel color to match the exact color of his eyes that I loved, but the reason I had gotten the shirt for him was because it had a picture of the state of Montana outlined on it. It had become an inside joke—well, actually more of an admittance—between the two of us that the only reason we ever were able to come together was because of our time in Montana. We joked that the state was now our sacred battle grounds. The fact that he was wearing this shirt felt like a silent signal that he was trying to yield. I accepted his signal with caution. "I texted you yesterday, but you didn't reply."

He raised his eyebrows. "I got your text. You said you wanted to talk before the funeral. I was busy trying to get a flight to come see you, but with the holiday, everything was booked up. I'm sorry but I obviously can't make it there."

"It's okay," I said, feeling a sting of loneliness. "I know it's a bad time of year to travel."

"My parents got a flight though."

"Really?"

"They said they already checked into the hotel and are getting ready. So, they'll be there if you need anything. You know my mom—" both his eyebrows raised in assurance "—she's ready to help."

I stared blankly ahead, trying to think of anything that Linda could help with, but my dad had arranged everything ahead of time. "That's sweet of them to come, but everything's ready." I searched his face on my screen for clues that he was mad at me, but I didn't see any telling signs. Anxiety screamed at me that he might hate me for the way I treated him the last few days and I blurted out, "I thought you were mad at me because you didn't reply to my text."

"No." He tilted his head forward. "I didn't reply because you haven't been replying to me for days. I figured it would be pointless."

"I know I avoided you." I lifted one shoulder into a cringe as I offered a quiet, "Sorry. I think I overreacted."

He gave me a half-smile as if he was trying to be supportive but was still confused. "It's okay."

"So . . ."

His forehead wrinkled slightly, and he leaned closer to the phone. "So, can we talk about this?"

I protectively pulled my phone further away from my face before I responded. "Yeah."

When I didn't add anything else, he asked, "Are you still upset?"

I wanted to open up to Fulton and to be able to confide in him the way I was always comfortable doing, but this felt like an

awkward job interview. The whole conversation was so unnatural.
I wasn't ready to jump right into the middle of it. *It wasn't fair.* I
had every right to be upset. I also had the right to take my time to
get over my hurt. I couldn't answer his simple question because it
wasn't a question that could be answered with a yes or no. After
silently tormenting myself with this issue for several moments, I
finally said, "It's more than that."

He lowered his chin and said, "I know."

"Do you?"

"I know I would be wounded if you had hidden something from
me." He closed his mouth and paused. Even through the phone,
I could feel his eyes searching my face for acceptance, but I was
stubborn and kept my mouth closed tightly. He continued, "I
know it was wrong. But I hope you see the bigger picture because
in a way, I was doing it *for you* and out of respect for your dad. Do
you honestly think you wouldn't have lied to me if the roles were
reversed?"

His question jolted me. I had been ready to lecture him on how
my heart felt fragmented by his lies, but I hadn't expected him
to play this kind of defense. I traced my tongue along the front
of my teeth while I thought. When I replayed our lives with a
role reversal, I wouldn't have thought twice about lying to him.
Back when my parents started our Montana journey, Fulton and
I weren't even on friendly speaking terms. We both knew that I
wouldn't have cared if he had gotten hurt from lies that my parents
could own. I swallowed hard and said, "I get that you did it for
what you thought were the right reasons."

"You do?"

"I do." My shoulders relaxed, and I went on, "I didn't at first, but I talked to Gabby. She also knew about my dad's diagnosis. Learning that was hard, but in a weird way it didn't bother me as much that she knew. When I broke it down, most of my anger toward you was more the shock of everything being revealed all at once." I took a second to think before adding, "And I know how convincing my dad is and how he must have sucked you into this whole thing. I can totally see my dad doing that. But . . ."

He leaned forward and softly repeated, "But."

"But it still hurts. A lot."

"I know it does." His eyes were unflinching as he confided, "The worst part is that when the whole thing started, you hated me. I wasn't worried how it would affect our relationship. I honored what your dad wanted and what my parents requested. I never for a moment thought you would feel hurt from me directly as a result of this. I thought your dad would explain everything, and if you had any hurt feelings, it would be toward him because he was the source." He held his hand up to pause himself. "I'm not saying I want you to be mad at him but that's how I thought about it then."

"I understand what you are saying."

"Good." He took a deeper breath, and then tacked on, "So, from my perspective, I hate that I was a part of it, but what I hate the most is that I hurt you. Never did I imagine that you and I would ever have come together in a friendship—let alone a romantic relationship—so I never thought about how I personally could hurt you."

Not having anything to add, I stayed quiet. He covered everything I needed to hear. That's the thing with him—he was always honest with me. Even when I was at the peak of my anger, deep down I always knew I could trust him. I lowered my eyes while I recounted his words. He admitted it was wrong, and I understood how he got dragged into it. After a while he added, "I would never lie to you, Abs."

I raised my eyes back to find his on the screen. "Promise?"

"Absolutely."

"And just to be clear," I started, "there is nothing else I need to know about, right? You might as well tell me now."

"No." He shook his head. "You know everything. No more secrets."

I exhaled, relenting all this drama. "Okay."

"Okay? Does that mean you aren't mad at me?"

"It means that I understand, and I believe that your intentions were not to hurt me."

He raised an eyebrow. "So, we are good?"

I smiled as sweetly as I could even though a tiny bit of me was wary but then the doorbell rang. I was so focused on our conversation that I had forgotten I had other stuff to do today. I sprang to my feet and said, "Hold on a second. Let me grab the door." I ran down the stairs and opened the door. With my phone still on a video call I let Kim inside. I watched her survey the room, and her eyes landed on my phone. When she saw Fulton's face, she leaned over to peer into my camera and waved at him. "Oh, Fulton, hi."

"Hi, Kim," he replied.

My brows lower dramatically when I gazed at Kim, who was smiling at Fulton. I turned my phone to exclude Kim from the shot, and I zoomed in on Fulton. Then I pointed to Kim. "Do you two know each other?"

Kim stayed relaxed like she didn't think it was a big deal, but Fulton automatically stiffened. "It's a—"

I cut him off. "Are you for real right now?" I glared at him through the phone. "Are you telling me you know my aunt?" I didn't give him time to reply. My mind was already racing, accusing him of more lies. "How on earth do you know my aunt? I only met her last week."

Kim looked at me and made a silent oh with her mouth like had been busted for something bad. Then she pivoted on her heel and turned to the door. "I can leave if I'm interrupting something."

I pointed at her with a sharp index finger. "No. You stay. I want to know how you two know each other. I don't remember telling you about him. When you walked in, I watched your eyes look at my phone. You recognized him. How?"

She lifted her face to peek at Fulton on my phone. "Do you want to explain this one?"

"I can," he said slowly.

"Please do," I said haughtily.

"I was at your parents' house . . ."

I pointed to the floor I was standing on. "You were here."

"I was. I came about a month ago to say goodbye to your dad."

I defensively put my free hand on my hip like I wasn't convinced. "Okay."

"My parents had said how sick he was." He tilted his head cautiously toward me. "You know that part. When I heard that the end was close, I felt I needed to see him to tell him goodbye and pay my respects. So, I went there on a weekend, stayed for a night, and that's when I met Kim. She came over to check on him, and we talked some."

"Oh, you talked, did you?"

Kim spoke up. "I don't see why you're upset, Abs. It's not a big deal that he came to visit."

"I'm upset because he literally just told me he didn't have any more secrets. He has never told me he came to visit my dad. I have spoken to him every day, sometimes multiple times a day, for the past six months. He would have had to call me from *this* house. Call me crazy, but I think it is sort of a big deal to not mention he was inside my parents' house."

Kim inched toward the door with tiny, quiet steps. "I'm going to go. I can see this is something you two need to discuss. I can meet you at the funeral home."

"I'm sorry, Kim." I followed her. "I really do need to come with you. I can't do this alone. I know we are cutting it close for time too." I looked back at Fulton on my phone. "I can't talk about this anymore right now. I have to go bury my dad." His mouth moved like he wanted to talk, but he respected my request and didn't press it.

"Okay," he agreed. I pretended not to notice the anguish in his eyes. He wanted to say more, but I clicked end on my phone call. While I watched his face disappear from my screen, I noticed my hand was squeezing my phone so tightly, it was white and clammy.

I grabbed my purse, tossed my phone into it, and ushered Kim out the door. Remembering I hadn't had time to comb my hair yet, I clumsily dug in my purse for a hair tie. "I guess it's going to be a ponytail day," I said as I groomed my hair back with shaky fingers. We walked down the pathway together, and I wiped the dampness from my hands on my dress while I silently thanked the Lord for the interruption in my call with Fulton. Everything was changing—no vanishing—so fast. I wanted to hit pause so I had time to think. That wasn't an option. So, an interruption that gave me time to process the change was greatly appreciated even if the interruption was burying my dad—before he also vanished for good.

Chapter Ten

Sitting in the church's front pew, sandwiched between Kim and her kids, wasn't exactly how my introverted self needed to grieve. I managed to pay attention to be respectful, but I mostly stayed numb over the emotional whiplash from the back and forth with Fulton and my dad's passing. With my heart tangled up in doubts about Fulton, I hadn't had time to even think about my dad this morning—which added to the guilt spearing my heart while I listened to a sermon about relating earthly fathers to our heavenly Father.

My dad had been pushing me hard these last couple of years to find my direction. I understood why, buy I still felt lost. His funeral definitely put me in a mood. I was ready to grieve, but I didn't want to do it in the front row where everyone could see me. I needed to be alone.

Since the ground was frozen, there was no burial today. When the service was over, everyone headed downstairs for a luncheon. I tried to ditch out the back door. Unfortunately, I wasn't fast enough because Linda saw me. "Are you leaving?"

"I need to." I stopped on the step, wrapping my coat tighter around my body, and I kept my face down while I tied the belt on my coat. "I understand it looks rude, but I need some time alone." I was flustered and fumbled with my purse strap.

She gently closed her lips, pulling them into a small reassuring smile. "Call me if you need anything."

Blinking back tears, I silently nodded, resenting the way she always reminded me of what a mother *should* be, and all that my mother never was. I didn't need my mother wound ripped open today. I held my hand up softly and waved goodbye while I spun on my heel to duck out the door. Then I walked briskly down the street, not knowing where I was even headed. Almost on cue in an uncanny way, my phone vibrated in my coat pocket. I knew before I looked that it was Fulton.

I pulled my phone out from my coat pocket and nervously tapped my thumb on my phone. As much as I had told myself to forgive him and give him another shot—and part of me needed him, especially now—another part of me was stuck in neutral. I could forgive him for the lies because I understood how he got into the mess, and I totally understood they were more my dad's lies, but I was struggling with all my memories.

I felt so cheated out of my past when I thought about how naturally Fulton and I had grown together in what I thought were genuine moments of us slowly trusting each other. Now all that was overshadowed, because he had this secret he had been covering up. It especially bothered me that after I had given him the chance to come clean and he said he didn't have any more secrets. Why didn't he tell me he went to my parents' house? Especially if he was there saying goodbye like he said he was. I didn't see any harm in that, or the need to keep it a secret. Unless he was doing something else? The whole thing was confusing enough on its own, but when it got jumbled up into this terrible timing with my family drama, it all caused an unprecedented tsunami of emotions that I couldn't deal with. I texted while I walked.

"I know you want to talk about this, but I think I need time."

Fulton: *"I understand, but I really wish we could talk."*

Me: *"I'm sure you do. I wish we could too, but I'm not okay today. I sort of want to just spend time grieving my dad and not thinking about this."*

Fulton: *"I understand that, but I'm starting to not like how we are leaving things. Is there something I can do to make this better?"*

I tapped my thumb on my phone as I pressured myself to be nicer to him, but I didn't have it in me right now.

I texted: *"Not right now."*

Fulton: *"Talk soon?"*

I looked away as soon as I read his request, I wasn't going to call him any time soon and I doubted if I would be able to answer any of his calls. Part of me knew I was being cruel, but I couldn't lie and tell him we were fine. We weren't. *I needed time.* I stuffed my phone back into my pocket. Things were changing between us, and it was happening too fast for me to understand. More than that, I honestly didn't care to understand right now because I missed my dad—immensely.

I flew back to Paris the next day fully aware that my life had done a complete one-eighty in one week. I had so much built-up angst in my gut that I had reverted to an old nervous habit of chewing my nails. I should have booked an appointment with a therapist but talking never did much but make it worse. Maybe I was an anomaly like that, but I needed to dance to get the pressure out. And since I couldn't dance, I spent the night watching ballets. It must have been an angel that pointed me to a new one when I found the original version of *The Dying Swan*. This was a different kind of death story than Romeo and Juliet. It was missing the anguish. It displayed a freedom that was painfully beautiful. It was like the swan had all his glories until his last moment and then rather than lose his beauty and get old, he just folded to fade.

The striking finality of the way the swan folded to his death caused me to grab my own chest as it felt like an arrow had literally been shot straight into my heart. Instead of piercing my fractured heart, it tacked the missing piece of information it needed to understand why my dad didn't tell me he was dying. I saw my dad's own strength in the swan's fold. Folding held a graceful dignity, and I now comprehended that he never wanted me to remember him as wounded. I was finally able to understand how my dad had left me out of his decisions, relieving me of some of the remorse I had been feeling. Then I drifted asleep, dreaming of a Yankee-hat-wearing swan dancing among the stars.

Chapter Eleven

An opened box of donuts on my desk with an obvious one missing greeted me when I walked into the office the next morning. "It's good to have you back," Gabby said.

I surveyed the office, feeling a little distant even though I hadn't been gone long. "I'm ready for some normal." I walked past the donut box, not tempted by the treat. My appetite had been missing for days. When I set my bag on my desk, my eyes got a glimpse of my phone inside. There was a new text from Fulton flashing on the front screen. I quickly zipped up the bag and pushed it further away from me to avoid thinking about him.

"Well, if you're looking for normal, then you aren't in the right place," Gabby teased as she crossed the room and sat on the corner of my desk.

I politely grinned, trying to soak up her sarcasm. I needed to forget all my torments in my heart. "Right. I forgot."

She cleared her throat. "In all seriousness, though, I'm glad you made it back safely. And I'm sorry about your dad."

I swallowed, forcing myself to gaze up at her. "Thank you. It's good to have a distraction." I hit the power button on my computer, and I then looked back at her. "I'm ready to work."

"Okay then." She reached over the aisle between our desks and retrieved a clipboard from her desk. "Do you really want to know what's on the giant to-do list?" Fanning through the pages, she showed me how huge it was. I usually had a page or two with tasks written on them, but there must have been a stack of twenty pages now. It was like all my work from the last two weeks didn't get done, and it was all stacked on the clipboard waiting for me. I knew Gabby was anxious for me to get stuff done, but I also knew we needed to have another kind of conversation first. Before I lost my nerve, I took a gamble that now would be the perfect time since, judging from her list, she obviously needed me. "Um, I do want to get back into work, but I was hoping to have a chat with you first."

"Sure." She set her clipboard down.

I leaned back in my chair and began to speak the words I had practiced: "You know I love working with you, and you have taught me so much." I waited, watching as her eyes grew rounder with interest. "You know my personal situation, and I also understand your professional situation and the arrangement we've had together has been wonderful—"

She interrupted me. "You're asking to get paid, aren't you?"

I chewed my lip and nodded.

"Well, you're right," she said. "I know your situation and you know mine. I love having you here, and I knew that once you didn't have your dad's financial support, you would need something from me. I understand that, and I think you deserve that."

I took a deep sigh of relief. "Ah, thank you. I was so nervous about this and how it was going to go. I wasn't sure what I was going to do—"

"Abs." She leaned forward, gently cutting me off again. "I'm sorry. Like I said, you deserve it, and you need it. It's what is fair for you. I went over my books, but I honestly don't see how I can do it right now. The wage I can afford wouldn't even be legal, let alone a livable wage for you."

I put my hand on my chest. "So, no?"

She shook her head, like she was trying to convince herself as well of the bad news. "I'm so sorry. I had hoped dearly that I could do this for you and to help honor your dad, but I can't swing it. I think the best thing for you right now is for me to let you go and help you find your way."

"What am I going to do?" I wondered out loud. It had never occurred to me, that I wouldn't have *this* life to go back to. This life with this job was the one thing that had still felt rooted in my life.

"You have so much talent," Gabby stated. "I'll write you the strongest know letter of recommendation. I know a ton of people in this industry, and it should be worth something. You will find something."

"But I don't want to find another job." I realized it was childish to even say it, but I couldn't handle anymore change. My breath was weak when I added, "I want to work for you."

"I know you do. I want that too, but it's not going to happen this time. You need a real job with real benefits, and I can't give that to you."

I rested my face in my hands and rubbed my forehead as I thought about having to find a new job. I was naïve that I hadn't realized this was going to be an issue until now. "So now what?"

"You want my advice?"

"Please. I don't know what to do."

"I think since your lease is paid at your apartment through the month, you stay here. I'll help you get your resume updated. We can reach out together to some contacts I have to see if there is anything opening up. But ultimately, you're going to have to consider moving back to the U.S. and finding an entry-level job there. At least you know the language there."

"I don't want to start over," I said softly, barely above a whisper.

"I know. I've tried to make this as fair as I can. I decided to pay for your plane ticket back to the States. I'll network my butt off for you to try to get you a paying gig, but other than that, I just can't."

I blinked a couple of times. I had honestly thought all my emotions were numb, but a new knot twisted in my gut. This one was whispering to me that I was going to fail on my own. My dad had always made all my connections for me. How was I going to do this so soon after his passing?

Gabby dropped her gaze to her pile of to-do lists but quickly shifted her gaze back to me. "I looked at your portfolio. It's strong, but what you don't have enough of is tangible samples. Your portfolio will get you an interview, but you're going to need physical samples to bring once you are in the door. I want to help you do this right, and you need to make samples. Why don't we start now."

I couldn't let my eyes abandon her stack of lists. She was relieving me of my duties, and she needed me badly. She was putting my needs ahead of hers. I appreciated her for it, but I also felt torn. She pointed to my computer screen to indicate that I should pull up my portfolio files, but I stalled and waited for her to look back at me. When she didn't, I knew this was as hard for her as it was for me—it was going to be a parting of friends. "Gabby," I said softly.

Her eyes shifted to meet mine. "Yeah?"

"Thank you."

She lowered her eyes humbly as if she were trying to not receive any credit for what she had done for me. "Honestly, the pleasure was all mine. I loved having you as my assistant. You are going to be missed." Her lips slid into a grin. "Now, let's see these designs of yours again. I'm thinking you need a killer special-occasions dress to add to your samples."

It wasn't until I grabbed my mouse to find my file that I realized my hands were shaking. I knew how incredibly blessed I had been to have been able to work with Gabby, but I also agreed with her. It was time for me to find my own job now, and it terrified me.

"That's the one." Gabby pointed to one of the dresses on my screen. "That's the one that is going to land you a job."

I followed her finger, and then I died a little inside. That was the dress I had designed to wear to Fulton's college graduation. My dad had helped me write the sell for it, calling it the perfect blend of sophisticated business and uptown class. It had a business silhouette with a lace overlay complete with feminine lace collar and flowy lace sleeve cuffs. I pursed my lips as I studied the details one more time. I had poured my heart into that design—it was admittedly my best work. Gabby was right. This was the dress that would help me stand out the most. I clicked on the dress to make it pop up bigger on the screen. Then I said, "Let's do this." A grin slid on my face in the first genuine grin I felt since my dad had passed, and a tinge of excitement bubbled in my gut for what the possibilities of my future would hold. Then I looked heavenward and quietly thanked my dad for that.

Chapter Twelve

One hectic, stressful week later, I was back in New York with
a string of interviews Gabby had helped me line up. Most of
them were for entry-level designer jobs, but I applied for a couple
assistant jobs to make sure I ended up with something. I figured at
this point I wasn't going to be picky because I needed to secure an
income. I had rented a room for the week with the little money I
had left in my bank account. The time clock of doom in my head
never let up on reminding me that once that money ran out, I
would have to stay at my mom's house. That consequence was the
best motivation ever to hustle my way into a paying gig.

At first, I had high confidence that everything would work out,
but my interviews were a lot tougher than I thought they would
be. Each designer who interviewed me spent a lot of time asking
about my formal education. Since I didn't have a degree, I tried to
do what Gabby had instructed me to do and focus on my portfolio
and samples. Unfortunately, I could tell that it wasn't enough
because most of my interviews ended shortly after that part of the
discussion.

One of the designers flat out told me I needed a degree, and she rudely showed the stack of resumes she had from designers who already had degrees. She told me to come back to apply after I finished college. The thing that bugged me the most was that the designers wouldn't even look at my portfolio. I knew that if they looked at my designs, they would see that I had the talent and experience to be successful.

The whole interview process ripped open my dad wound even more because he would have been able to help me form a pitch for my skills to support me through this process. I scolded myself for not paying better attention to his advice when I had the chance. When I finished the last of my interviews on Friday, I was relieved to be done with my hustle while also scared out of my mind. Now all I had to do was wait for my destiny to unfold . . .

I had my room rental through the weekend, and I thought about catching up with some of my friends. I hadn't spoken to Tina or Becky since Gabby's dress turned up torn. Even though I didn't know for sure it was one of them, I had convinced myself it was. I mostly suspected Tina. I had planned on texting Becky because I missed her, but instead I found myself unexpectedly wondering—maybe out of habit or curiosity—about the comedy club.

It was weird to think about going to the comedy club by myself, but I had been through so much this last month, and I needed to laugh. I remembered that when I left New York last spring that Wally had started a headline Saturday comedy show I checked online, and he was on the schedule. Without hesitation I booked a ticket, and then to pass the time, I handwrote thank-you notes to all the people who had interviewed me that week. That was one of those special touches my dad had always insisted on, and I was now hanging on to every word of his I could remember.

Antsy for the time to pass, I left as soon as I could, knowing if I didn't force myself to be busy, I would start googling tragic ballets again. Although I didn't think there was anything wrong with spending hours watching the same tragedy over and over to help me grieve, I knew I needed to try to be in a better mood—at least sometimes. I also felt strongly about having a positive attitude while I went through the interview process.

I easily found my way back to the theatre and took a seat near the front against the wall. I peeked at the VIP table where we all used to sit to see if I recognized anyone, but I didn't. Seeing this room made me reflect on the past year. I painfully remembered how I had spent most of my year trying to get Fulton to notice me. *Now I was avoiding him.* What would say if he knew I was back in town and didn't call him?

Before I could get too melancholy, Wally walked on stage. The fashionista in me quickly took notice that he had leveled-up his wardrobe. He still wore his normal jeans, but I could tell from where I was sitting that they were expensive. He also wore a preppy sweater and collared shirt, reminding me of how his dad used to dress. I smiled, musing over how he was basically turning into a mini version of his dad. As for his act, it was obvious he had honed his craft over the last year, even adding in a ventriloquist doll who outsmarted him about everything, and the routine had me in stitches.

I thought I laughed as much as I could considering my current mood, but I was wrong because the headline comedian who came on after Wally was even better. Never having heard of her before, I wasn't expecting much especially when I saw she was a blue-haired elderly lady. However, she was an expert impressionist who spent some time ridiculing modern fashion. I died at least three times at the obnoxious way she swung her dress while impersonating models. It was so stinking spot on, I regretted I hadn't recorded it to send to Gabby.

After the show, I loitered in the back, hoping to get a glimpse of Wally. Just when I was leaving out the back door, I heard a voice behind me call, "Ab Machine!"

My lips instantly curled while I turned back around and shouted, "Wally!" I took a few steps toward him until we were close enough for me to lean in for a friendly hug. "Great show. I laughed the whole time."

"Good. You were supposed to."

I waved my hand toward the scattered people still lined up to exit. "It was a packed house. How'd you see me?"

"I recognized you while I was up there, but the lights were so bright I swore they were playing tricks on me. I thought you were supposed to be in Paris, so I was pretty sure I was losing it. However, I had to run up to the projector room to get some contracts. I peeked out to recheck, and there you were."

I pointed to the window in the upstairs wall. "Oh, so you spied on me from your secret projector room?"

"I forgot I showed you up there." His mischievous grin widened, and I recollected how it had gotten us into a few predicaments. I used to get nervous when he would flash that smile at me, but now after not having seen it in so long, it put me at ease. "That was fun." He chuckled, then added, "Good ol' stalking-Fulton days."

He stopped, leaned his head to look behind me and asked, "Where is he anyway?"

Lifting one shoulder very casually, I said, "I don't know."

He bucked an eyebrow. "I assumed he came with you. So, you're here by yourself . . ."

"I am." I didn't want him to ask me about Fulton again, so I diverted quickly and said, "I'm actually in town for the week for interviews. My apprenticeship with Gabby ended this week It's time for me to fly solo and get a job."

"Oh," was all he said. I chewed my bottom lip, hoping my explanation was enough. It must have been because he said, "What kind of jobs are you looking for?"

"Technically, I've been training to be a designer, and that's my end goal, but I'm looking for anything really. I've applied for assistant jobs, but heck, who knows, if I don't get a call back this week, I might be applying to be a janitor somewhere."

"If you have janitor skills you need to unleash, let me know." He tilted his head forward to playfully pry. "I've been looking for help cleaning."

I started to relax into the conversation and let my arms cross over my chest to rest. "I thought you had a guy who cleaned here."

"My dad had a guy who worked for him for years, but when he retired last fall, that guy decided it was also time to retire too."

"Does that mean you are managing everything now?"

He slowly nodded. "It does. He has been training me for the last year, but it's official now." He placed a hand on the seat next to him and stated, "This boat is mine. My dad still helps me balance the books at the end of the month to make sure we are making money. I'm the one who has to drive the business all month long."

"That shouldn't be too hard." I pursed my lips slightly when I remembered how packed this place was especially on college night. It wasn't in the best location, but since it was Off-Broadway, it was substantially more affordable, especially for people who wanted to come regularly. "It seems like it's been well established, and every show I've been to is filled."

Wally scratched the back of his head. "It is established, but there is a lot that has changed in entertainment especially with internet streaming being so cheap. It's getting harder to pack a show because it's so easy to stay home and binge-watch on the couch."

"I can see that being an issue," I agreed, as it reminded me of the many conversations that Gabby and I had about how the internet had changed fashion.

"It's tough, but I believe in this place." He scanned the room, and his eyes sparkled like he was absorbing a lifetime of memories. "The internet's great but communities need a place like this to come together."

"I don't think you'll have any problem running it."

"I'm going to give it my best shot." He let his eyes linger on mine as if to confirm his conviction. Then he shifted the conversation by asking, "So do you need a ride home?"

"No." I adjusted my bag on my shoulder when I remembered the theatre was closing, and I should be leaving. "I rented a room a few blocks away so I'm fine walking."

"Are you sure?"

"Yeah, I was planning to stop and grab dinner on the way home anyway, so I'll be fine."

"Dinner? It's ten thirty."

I grinned, feeling like a tourist with a weird meal schedule. "I'm still on European time. Ten is pretty average for dinner over there."

He playfully touched his stomach. "Man, I'd be so fat if I ate that late every night."

"No, you wouldn't, especially not if you were like me when I was working. Ten would be the first time I would sit down since lunch."

"Well, it was great seeing you. Say hi to Fulton for me. It's been a while since he's been in, and I've been so swamped with work I haven't had much time to reach out to him."

My mouth got dry when I thought about the many texts from Fulton that were sitting on my phone screen unread. I forced a smile and said, "I'll tell him when I talk to him." I took a step toward the exit, and to make sure he didn't ask me about Fulton again, I switched the conversation back to him. "What are you going to do now?"

"Me?" He glanced quickly around the room again that still had people chatting in scattered groups. "I'm going to wait until this place empties out and then lock up and go to bed. I have to be back at six to clean."

"Clean?"

"Yeah, I told you I'm looking for a janitor. Until I find one, there isn't anyone else to do it. Normally I'd stay late to clean up, but I'm shot." He rubbed his eyes like he was reminding himself how tired he was. Then with a yawn he added, "I'll start fresh in the morning."

"You really are working hard."

"I gotta give it my best shot. I want to make my insanely demanding dad proud." His smile said he was both enjoying the journey and overwhelmed at the same time.

His comment reminded me so much of Gabby and how hard we would work and the silly excuses she would come up with to justify her insanity. "My old boss would always call it baptism by fire."

His head swayed in agreement. "Yep, that's definitely accurate. There is no honeymoon around here." He was still smiling, but it was evident through his wavering eyelids that he was tired. Remembering how long my workdays with Gabby used to feel, I took my cue to leave and placed my hand on his lower arm and said, "It was good to see you. I'll let you go so you can finish your work."

"It was great to see you too," he replied, and then added, "Stop in again."

I stepped forward and called, "I'll definitely stop in. Hopefully I can get a job and stay here."

"Right."

I waved one last time before letting myself out the door and headed down the street. I wasn't more than a block away when I felt my phone vibrate again. I dug into my purse, already knowing it was Fulton lighting up my phone. He had been regularly sending me goodnight texts. It had always been something I had looked forward to and appreciated, but now I sort of forgot what the point of them was. Since I knew it was just a safe goodnight text, I opened it and read it, confirming that it was exactly that and nothing more. Usually, these texts came at off- hours since I was in Paris, but tonight was the first time we had shared the same time zone in months, with him being just a short commute away to his school on Long Island. A month ago, I would have died knowing we were this close. Part of me pined for him, wanting to text him that I was in the city and had time to see him. But the bigger part of me was massively confused, knowing if I saw him now, it would make my confusion worse. My heart was pretty clear in telling me that I wasn't ready to get over my hurt. So, I returned my phone to my pocket and walked home.

Chapter Thirteen

It wasn't a conscious decision—more of a reflex that was rooted in lack of sleep and deep anxiety—but somehow, I found myself outside Wally's theatre again. It was still one of those crazy early morning hours where the rising sun reflected off the sides of the buildings, creating long shadows on the sidewalk. Most New Yorkers weren't even out of bed yet, but here I was loitering around in front of the familiar brick building, trying to think of a reason to go inside. I didn't want to act like a stalker, but I couldn't think of a reason to just drop in for a friendly visit. After playing with a few excuses, I decided to give in to my awkwardness and call him.

"Um, hello," he answered, sounding like he just woke up.

"Good morning!" I let my voice ring with cheer into the phone. "Um, surprise, but I'm standing outside."

"Ha! Joking."

"No, for real," I said, feeling like a dork. Then he stayed mute for way too long for me to be comfortable with my imposition. It made me wonder if he thought I was a crazy stalker, so I lowered my voice to give him an explanation he would accept. "I couldn't sleep because I was stressed about my job interviews. So, I went for a walk and ended up here."

"Um, okay," he finally said, still not sounding convinced. "Give me a sec to come down. I'll let you in."

I leaned against the brick wall, feeling like an absolute tool for considering this to be a good idea. Not knowing what I was thinking, but it only dawned on me now that Wally might be talking to Fulton. I couldn't imagine what Fulton would do if he knew I was in town, still ignoring him. Anxiety crept into my throat again, and my fingers twitched, craving something to do. I commanded my feet to walk and go home, but before they would listen, Wally opened the door.

I cringed when I saw he was wearing sweatpants and a crinkled t-shirt that looked like he had slept in it. His hair still had a serious case of bedhead, and I could have sworn I saw a tinge of dried drool glisten on his chin. He obviously wasn't expecting company at the crack of dawn. I reprimanded myself for inviting myself in, but he quickly put me at ease with his mischievous smile. "I know I'm irresistible and all," he started teasing, "but normally I have to at least offer free food to get the cute girls to hang out with me."

My cheeks heated, not because of his taunting but because I saw how odd this visit looked. I walked through the heavy door and defended myself. "I have insane anxiety right now being unemployed. I needed to do something to keep me busy, and there isn't anything else to do this early." Then I silently prayed he'd drop how weird this seemed. Motioning to his janitor cart pushed against the wall, I added, "Plus, I'm amazing at helping people clean, and I can totally help you."

He rubbed his forehead. "I haven't been getting much sleep either. We must have the same case of anxiety."

"It must be going around," I affirmed as I walked toward the cart and pointed to a spray bottle. "Dusting is my superpower."

"Go for it." He showed me his easy grin. "You can wipe all the chairs down, and I'll follow with the mop."

I walked to the first row of seats and started to wipe the arm rests down, remembering how I had performed a similar cleaning duet with Fulton last year when I was obsessed with him. There must be something wrong with me that I don't have normal social skills and go around begging people to let me clean with them for attention. Then I accidentally touched gum, still sticky and moist from last night, stuck underneath an arm rest. I gagged and looked at Wally, who chuckled as he pointed to the cart. "There's a razor on the cart."

"This is gross." I moved to retrieve the razor and wrinkled my nose when I went in for the attack.

He pointed accusingly at me. "Too late to quit now."

"No, I didn't mean it like that. It's just . . ." I surveyed the room, taking in how large it was for two people to clean. "This is a huge room to clean. I can't believe you do this by yourself. Doesn't anyone need a job?"

"I've had a couple of applicants, but they want more money than I want to pay them. For now, I'm going to try to keep it up by myself."

I kept my head down while I wiped chairs off as fast as I could, and I asked another question to avoid an awkward silence. "Has business been that slow?"

He sloshed the mop behind me, making a water arc that barely missed my feet. "It's not really slow. It's more that I would rather spend the money on other investments right now."

"Other investments? That sounds intriguing."

He snickered. "Nah, not really intriguing, but it is fun."

"Do tell."

Replacing the mop in the soap bucket just along enough for him to rinse it, he then turned back to me. "I had this idea to increase our reach. It's been a lot of work, but I'm hoping it'll pay off."

"That's pretty vague. You're not thinking about anything illegal, are you?"

"No." His eyes lit up from the joke. "I save all the illegal stuff for the weekends."

"That's good." My shoulders eased as we fell into our friendly rhythm. It felt good to be on my feet, doing something to keep busy as well as forcing my mind to think about something that wasn't causing me near-mental breakdowns. I pressed on. "So?"

He lifted the mop again, wringing it out. "You know how those cheesy Christmas movies are becoming a major thing, and they are everywhere in December?"

"Yeah." I bobbed my head. "I've seen the ads. They are mostly the same plot with different embarrassing sweaters and new fun Christmas names like Jon Tinzleberry."

He gestured to me with an energy that showed his enthusiasm. "See! You know exactly what I'm talking about. They are everywhere. It's a huge demographic," he explained. "Well, I needed a way to compete with internet streaming, and that's one of the largest categories of shows streamed in December. So, I had this brainstorm. What if I booked a live production of something like that? The idea snowballed from there. I wrote a script, got some actors from the nearby acting school, and we are all set to go next week."

"You wrote a play?"

"I did." He scratched the top of his head. "That was the easy part, actually. I'm used to writing scripts, because I do it every week for my comedy. However, it turns out building a set and directing people are basically like a modern military torture program." Then he dramatically held his hands up and pretended he was going to strangle someone. It made me smirk and he continued, "Had I known how hard it was going to be, I would not have even attempted it." Then he let out a noisy breath and said, "But at this point, I'm committed."

My smile genuinely pulled up more. "That is so amazing. I had no idea you had that kind of talent. But now that I think of it, Fulton did say a few weeks ago that he went to a play here. Was that along the same lines?"

"Sort of. It's getting harder to book the headlining acts because they are so expensive. The seats hardly ever sell out because there is so much free content online now. The only way we're making money is to have cheap or free performances. We can sell cheap tickets by the boatloads because people are always looking for something free or cheap to do. Then we make money on concessions. Now my aim is to get people in the door even if we must give away tickets. So, I've been experimenting with all low-cost theatre productions."

I was about to tell him what a good idea he had, but before I could, he abruptly sloshed his mop back in the bucket and squaring his body in front of me. "Are you okay?"

I was so taken back by his directness, my entire head bounce backwards. "Um, what?"

His head tilted slightly to the side as he continued to peer directly into my eyes. "It's fine and everything, but I'm having a hard time understanding why you have such an interest in my business." Pointing to my rag, he added, "And I know cleaning this place for free isn't exactly fun." Then he took a small step forward. "What's really going on?"

I lowered my eyes defensibly. "Why do you think something is going on?"

He made a grandiose shrug with his lips ajar like he was speechless. Neither one of us filled in the silence with words. I knew I was busted, but the crazy thing was that I didn't know exactly what I was busted for. Yes, I had been sad and upset, but I didn't think that was a crime. I was overly anxious and desperate for something to do to keep busy, and yes, I was avoiding some things but that didn't exactly mean anything was wrong with me. Wally stared at me, and I knew he saw right through me. I relented and shrugged, saying, "I don't know what is wrong with me. A lot, maybe."

I expected him to laugh at my hopelessness the way he always effortlessly made a joke out of everything, but instead he took another step closer and put a friendly arm on my shoulder. "Can I guess?"

"Okay," I answered weakly, now totally intrigued by what was going on in his head.

"You're mad at Fulton."

I quickly looked away to avoid him seeing a recognition in my eyes. "Nah, why would you think that?"

"Um, because he lives a couple hours away, and instead of going to see him, you are showing up here. Like I said before, I'm flattered, but the last time you hung out with me so much was when you were upset that he wasn't noticing you. It's sort of a pattern of yours."

I carefully licked my lips while I fought back the urge to deny it all. There wasn't a reason to fight my feelings anymore because Wally could see right through my lies. "Yeah, I'm confused." I rigidly squeezed my lips, knowing that wasn't the whole truth. "And I'm mad."

"And you're avoiding him too."

My brow lowered and I felt my anger bubble. "I am avoiding him," I defended. "But I don't think there is anything wrong with that. There is no rule that says if you are upset at someone you have to constantly look at them."

He let out a small chuckle. "No, there is no rule like that. That would be dumb."

"Right," I agreed. "And besides, I don't know what I would say to him right now. It doesn't seem fair to avoid him, but I need some time to know what I'm thinking."

"I understand. So, why are you mad at him? Maybe I can help."

I parted my lips. Explaining this was going to be harder than algebra. Wally knew nothing about my real life, about my mom's mental health issues, or about my dad's illness. I couldn't unload all that on him. Instead of confessing, I shrugged. "It's complicated. You wouldn't be able to understand."

"You can try."

Sighing loudly, I fumbled for a beginning spot to my story. This was going to take a while, so I sank down into the nearest chair and said, "There is a lot that went on, but when we moved to Montana, my parents gave me a few bogus reasons as to why we moved. I was mostly led to believe we moved to help my mom." I stalled then looked back at him, ready to receive judgement as I finished my thought. "My mom is crazy."

His face was unwavering when he replied, "You say that like it's a death sentence."

"The Montana part?"

"No, the part about your mom."

My eyes swelled in overwhelm. "That's exactly how it feels for me. My mom's insanity has ruined my life."

"Do you think that's fair?" His forehead now wrinkled in a surprising defensiveness.

"How do you know what's fair for me?"

Taking a small step back like he was taking himself out of a potential argument, he then redirected the conversation, "So anyway, you thought you were moving because of your mom. How does that add up to anything that would make you upset at Fulton?"

I momentarily closed my eyes, willing myself to shut down any annoyance, and I started my story again. "So, we moved, and then my mom got sick, so the move never helped her. I started to question why we couldn't move back since the move wasn't working. No one said anything to clarify things, and I continued to believe we were there because of my mom."

I stopped, wishing desperately that's where the story stopped, because that's where everything stopped making sense to me. I didn't want to talk about anything that happened next, not because it was confusing, but it wasn't fair! It was then that I saw what was bothering me become unveiled. I felt ghosted by my family. They failed to include me in one of the most important and intimate moments a family could go through. *It infuriated me!*

My eyes narrowed when I was finally able to speak. "The truth of the whole thing is that we moved to Montana because my dad was dying of cancer. Everyone knew about his illness, including Fulton—but not me." I watched his face, but it didn't convey what he was thinking, "My dad excluded me from any knowledge because he wanted me to spend the last year learning to be an adult." I shuddered and added, "It's embarrassing that everyone knew he thought I was too immature to deal with it." My eyes fell to the mop bucket before me. "But my dad passed a couple weeks ago, and the truth came out. Everyone knew, but I had been left out. If I said I was mad at Fulton for lying to me, that would be a lie because it's worse than that I'm totally gutted." I slowly raised my eyes as I was ready to hear what sage advice he had for me, but my confession quickly ended in vanity as we were interrupted by the sound of several people loudly walking through the theatre doors. One of the loudest people in the group, a fair-skinned male shouted, "Good morning, Walls."

Wally's eyes remained on mine, and I could feel an angst that hadn't been there earlier. Then he blinked and quickly turned to the group, calling out, "Morning, why don't you guys sit down and run lines to scene one. I'll be over in a sec."

When he turned his attention back on me, he still had deep empathy on his face but before he had a chance to circle back to my story, I said, "I get it. Your people are here."

Holding up a gentle hand to stop me from getting up and leaving, he explained, "It's rehearsal, but we can go upstairs if you want to talk some more . . ."

"Nah." A cooling rose in my chest like I was being let out of the hot seat, but I also noticed a feeling of loneliness creep in. Wally must have had superpowers that picked up on it because, before I could excuse myself, he said, "You know, now that I think of it, I could really use your opinion on what I have going on here." He gestured to the stage now littered with actors. "You have a background in performance." I started to shake my head no, but he pressed on and insisted, "Come on, please. I can't believe I never thought about it before, but it will mean a lot to me if you'd stay to watch and give me some feedback."

I knew the game he was playing. He could tell I was sad, and he didn't want me to be alone right now, but he also knew I was going to lie through my teeth to get out of admitting it. He knew if he acted like he needed help from me that I wouldn't be able to say no. I rubbed the back of my neck, wondering what I was getting myself into, but he was offering the exact thing I needed—a distraction. "I can stay for a little while if you want."

"Perfect. You can sit in the front row and tell me how terrible I am at this, and how it's going to be a huge flop."

"That sounds great," I joked. "Do I get popcorn?"

His smile was overly stretched, telling me he was trying hard to cheer me up, but nonetheless, I appreciated it. "I wouldn't want it any other way." He held out his fist, inviting me to bump his. "Deal?"

I met his fist with mine and chimed, "Let's do this."

Chapter Fourteen

"So, I think I got the basic story line to your play." I leisurely sat on the theatre stage with my feet hanging over the edge. The actors had all left, and the theatre was once again empty except for the two of us. "Cute and available flannel-shirt-wearing mechanic lives in adorable wintry town. A bakery-tycoon hag can't stand the cuteness of the town but uses its rural location to hoard and hide ingredients as well as build cheap factories as part of her mission to dominate the specialty macaroon market. She has a deep-rooted greed and dislike for anything that isn't work, especially holidays, because it causes her employees to ask off work and she spends those days alone. Then when an unforeseen world-wide shortage of flour causes the bakery industry to hoard all the available flour for necessities like bread, the world has no flour for Christmas cookies this year and all is lost!" I dramatically swept my hand across my forehead and faked weeping. "Hag, in all her greed, has an opportunity to help humankind because she had hoarded granary bins full of flour in her secret rural location." I paused, took a breath, and asked, "How am I doing?"

"Good so far."

"So, then bakery hag's greed comes to a boiling point when glue makers offer her millions of dollars for the coveted flour. Christmas-themed protestors beg her to not sell the flour for glue, but she only sees money. She flies to a small town, and while on her way to meet her glue connoisseurs, she accidentally bumps into an older man who has a white beard, and his name is Sam Closs." I snickered at how cheesy yet on point this storyline was. "Sam asks bakery tycoon to make Christmas cookies for the tree-lighting party in the town square, and she laughs in his face. When she does, she notices a weird twinkle in his eyes that leaves her speechless, and she runs off. That night as she sleeps, elves sneak into her bakery and set up her production line to mass produce Christmas cookies instead of her signature macaroons.

"She finds the cookies in the morning and is furious! She calls hot flannel-wearing-mechanic to fix the machines, but he fails as the machines seem to be locked under a secret code. In her fit of greed-fueled rage, she notices how sweet flannel-shirt-wearing mechanic is as he offers her a cookie that he had plucked off one of the lines. She bites into it, and as it melts in her mouth, it also melts the greed in her heart. She instantly falls in love with flannel-shirt guy, and together they collect the cookies and hand them out to everyone at the town square Christmas party." I sighed, then added, "The end."

Wally wrinkled his nose. "Too cheesy?"

"Not at all. It has the perfect amount of cheesy Christmas themes, an incognito Santa, and swoony love. I'd say you covered all your bases except for one thing."

A worry line traced on his forehead. "What did I miss?"

I gave him a small smirk to put him at ease. "You have the cheesy stuff down." I waved my hand in front of the stage set built up with a wintry town back drop. "But you need to elevate the ambiance to make it look theatrical."

He furloughed his eyebrows. "And you know how to do this?"

"I do," I bragged, knowingly. "You need some ballerinas."

"It's not a ballet," he replied dryly.

I held my finger up to stop his insults. "Trust me on this. You need to get ballerinas to play the part of the elves."

His eyes swept the stage as if he was imagining how it would look to have ballerinas dance the part of the elves. After a moment, his furloughed brow relented. He looked back at me and said, "It sounds like you are volunteering to help me on this."

"I can put together some choreography, and I know a few gals from my old dance company who would be perfect. I can ask them if you want me to."

"That sounds awesome and all, but can you get it done in a week?"

I bobbed my head as I weighed his request. "I've got nothing else to do."

"Okay, then I'll trust that you'll manage that part." He paused before asking, "Is there anything else missing?"

"Hmm," I thought out loud. "The flannel shirt is totally on point, but we could do better with some of the wardrobe. If this is going to be a Christmas production, let's level up the glamour. I can ask Gabby to sponsor this and get you hooked up with some fun scarves and swag for the townspeople."

His eyes widened. "Really? You would do that?"

"Sure, Gabby's always looking for exposure, and she loves helping me. Plus, my dad always said if you don't have a platform of your own, you need to find great partners to borrow from until yours takes off. We could totally use her name in the plug for your advertising."

"I haven't done much advertising except for how it's listed on our website," Wally admitted. "I'm trying not to spend any money on advertising since the whole point is to keep it low cost. I was going to get a poster outside this weekend so when we book the house for our weekend comedy shows, they'll see this play too."

My brow wrinkled. "Do you really think that is your target audience? I would think comedy goers aren't going to be the same people who get all googly-eyed for swoony Christmas stories."

Wally shot me a suspicious glance. "So now you're a marketing manager?"

"No, I'm not, but my dad was." I mindfully lowered my eyes, feeling a sting. "I've overheard him coach clients." *Ugh*, I winced. I had done so well at forgetting about my dad by being busy the whole morning. The sadness washed over me like high tides. *Man, do I miss him.* His presence was in everything I did. It was impossible to get the emotional break I desperately needed. But it wasn't only the emotions, it was everything. Always having the best advice, he would know exactly what Wally should do to pack his theatre again. Moving on without him was going to be so much harder than I had thought in so many ways—it was an impossibility.

"Are you okay?" Wally had a concerned look on his face, and something told me he had been talking to me, but I hadn't heard a word he had said. I swallowed to redirect my thoughts when my alarm on my phone interrupted me, startling us both. I retrieved my phone from my pocket, turned off the alarm. I was officially summoned to my one-way train ride to *my mom's house of insanity*. I had been putting off the thought all day, but I had reached my final hour where I needed to leave to make the last train back to Virginia. Out of money with no job offer, I was officially out of time. I stared unceasingly without offering an explanation. When Wally's patience wore off, he finally asked, "What's going on?"

I tucked my phone back into my pocket. "I gotta leave." I slid off the stage, stood in front of him, and said, "I forgot I don't, I . . ." I ran my fingers through my hair as I tried to think of a better word than to tell him I was homeless. My dad would have had a positive way to spin this. Ugh. *Now I'm thinking of my dad again.* My palms quivered, and I quickly hid them behind my back.

"Abs." Wally lowered his voice. "I'm so confused right now. What's wrong?" He pointed to my trembling hands. "This, what you're doing right now. That's not about Fulton. There must be something else going on. What's bothering you?"

I pressed my hands hard on my eyes to stop the building pressure, and I refocused myself. When I was calm, my hands dropped to my sides, and I locked eyes with Wally since I knew he wasn't letting me off any hooks here. "I'm moving back to my mom's house for a while until I get a job. I don't have the money to keep staying in the city. I'm just super bummed because my mom's a giant psycho, and it always stresses me out to have to be with her."

"Wait a second." He rested his finger on his chin. "You have to leave town."

I nodded somberly. "I want to come back, but I need a job first."

He motioned to the stage in front of him. "How are you going to help me with the elves if you are in Virginia?

"Oh, don't worry about that." I waved my hand in a dismissing way. "I can manage all that virtually. It's not a big deal, and it'll give me something to do to keep me occupied." His frozen face showed how unimpressed he was, so I affirmed my statement. "Trust me, I need something to do. It's not an issue. It'll get done."

His next words were slow while he selected them carefully. "Um, okay. But it sounds like you don't really want to go there." Then he lowered his voice a level like he was trying to tiptoe with his words. "Do you need a place to stay?"

My eyes grew with curiosity. "Are you offering?"

He lifted one shoulder. "There's a small dressing room backstage that has a couch in it. It's nothing fancy, but it's not being used. You're welcome to crash a few nights until you get things figured out."

The Everest-sized load of dread that was sitting on my shoulders started to immediately melt away. I searched his face for clues that he wasn't giving me a pity offer, and all I saw was him being genuine. I didn't want to become a total mooch, so I countered, "It sounds great, but I don't have any money to pay you. The only way I'll stay is if you let me help you clean."

"You don't have to twist my arm on that." His grin eased back onto his face, then he added, "Maybe you want to look at the space first to see if you'll be comfortable. It's pretty dated."

I gave him a stale expression. "You could show me outside to a back alley infested with rats, but as long as you'd be okay with me sleeping there, I'd prefer that overstaying with my mom." I grinned widely expecting him to chuckle, but instead he lowered his brow, waited a few quiet moments, then changed the subject.

"Okay, come on back. I'll show you the room." I followed him back through the side stage exit, the whole time watching the side of his face as he stayed quiet. If I hadn't known better, I would have thought something was bothering him. I knew he was okay with me staying here, so that wasn't it. It had to be something that was provoked by something I had said. What did I say wrong?

Chapter Fifteen

"So, like I said, it's pretty old and I haven't exactly cleaned back here in a while, or like ever really." Wally ran his finger along the top of a dressing table which completely soiled his finger in dust. "But you're welcome to stay." Then he brushed his hand on the front of his jeans and added, "Obviously, you can clean it up and do what you need to make it comfortable. This was my Nana's private room, and we never felt like opening it up for any public use. We sort of forget about it on our cleaning rotations."

If the cold and filth of the room had been depressing, it was immediately overshadowed by the mention of this room having been dear to Nana. I imagined her sitting at the dressing table in one of her Dior gowns, elegantly brushing her hair before a show. I no longer saw the dirt-stained curtains that looked like rags, but instead my vision locked in a weird time warp. I saw the fabric for what it had been back when it was originally hung—luxurious pearl-white-silk. "I love it," I said as I hugged myself, both to warm my body in the dampness of the room and to protect my emotions.

"You do?" Wally asked with a quizzical look on his face.

"Yea, it reminds me of Nana and her timeless dresses." I let my ballet bag drop onto the Queen Anne sofa. Thankfully that had been covered with a sheet. At least that would be something I could sleep on. "This isn't a dressing room," I defended dreamily. "It's part of Nana's legacy, and I'd be honored to stay here, and of course, I'll clean it up."

"Okay." As he turned to walk back out the door, he winced as if still confused by my situation. "I'll let you get set up in here then. I need to get back into the storage room to check on our food delivery that was dropped off. So, if you need anything, that's where I'll be."

I didn't want to make a big deal about what was happening. I was sure that to any outsider, someone like me—who just a few weeks ago had worked in Paris for a famous fashion designer and was now willing to basically sleep in filth—had to look desperate. The thing was that I didn't have a lot of pride left—okay, I had zero pride left. I *was* desperate. I was also extremely appreciative of how Wally had been generous while also sensitive to my situation and not making this embarrassing. So, before he slipped all the way out the door, I called after him, "Thank you."

Instead of saying, "You're welcome," he surprised me and took a step back into the room. "It's really not my business what's going on in your life." He scratched the side of his head, and I now recognized that as his confused fidget. "And, I'll keep this a secret." He pointed to the couch. "If you can be respectful about what I'm going to share . . ."

I inclined my head to better hear what was happening. Wally had removed all his normal foolishness from his face, and he was looking way too serious. "I can keep a secret."

He stared at the ceiling for a moment before continuing. "I know everyone sees me as the funny guy all the time, but there's more than one side to me. And when you talk about your mom, um, you know, how she has mental health issues . . ." I felt my lip's part defensively, but he continued. "I know what it's like."

I wasn't exactly sure what he was admitting to. Was he saying that his mom was also crazy? I had met his mom, and she seemed completely normal. He must have seen my confusion and offered clarification by saying, "I've struggled my whole life with a sort of bi-polarism. And without getting into it, I would want to say to anyone that's around someone with mental health issues that *we know we're hard to love.* We want to be better, but that desire makes the cycle more extreme. It's never our intention to hurt those people who love us. "

The stillness that loomed in the room was agonizing. I couldn't understand if he was reprimanding me for speaking disrespectfully about my mom, or if he had felt personally offended because of how he identified with my criticisms. Nonetheless, I immediately had a heightened self-awareness about all the ways I had spoken about my mom in what I thought was a casual detached way. Now I saw in retrospect how when I had joked about her, Wally had never laughed and usually changed the subject. I internally wrestled with the notion of whether I owed him an apology, but I could tell by the sincerity on his face that an apology wasn't something that he was searching for. If I read his facial expression correctly, he was trying to spread a little understanding and compassion around—which I had clearly lacked. I was at a loss for words and despite feeling insanely guilty, I ditched the idea of an apology and spoke as truthfully as I could. "I didn't know."

"It's okay. I wouldn't expect you to know. I'm not sure why I told you, but when you joke about your mom, your jokes aren't funny. All I can feel is that you're obviously hurt by her. I'm guessing that's where the avoidance is coming from, but I thought maybe I could help you understand there is suffering on the other side too."

My mind was already racing, trying to decipher the way I was going to talk my way out of this one, but Wally didn't give me a chance to reply. He simply slipped out of the room, leaving me stunned with a new light shining on my attitude. It didn't make me feel good. In fact, I felt horrible.

Chapter Sixteen

A fast week later, time had dwindled down to a remaining three hours before the curtain opened on our first night of our Christmas drama. Sitting on a stool behind the ticket counter, I watched Wally close out the reservation screen on his computer and announce, "It's official. We are *sold* out of tickets." Then he looked at me and added, "I have no idea how you did it, but we'll have a full house tonight for the first time in a long time."

My eyelashes fluttered as I looked down at my phone sitting next to me. On the front screen flashed a text from Monica, my dad's old colleague, confirming her marketing email blast had been completed. I hadn't planned on calling her; I wanted to do this on my own—like my dad had wanted me to be able to. However, I had a moment of panicked reflection where I remembered that even though my dad did want me to be able to stand on my feet, he had also left a trail of people who were willing and *wanted* to help me. In my effort to be helpful to Wally, I had reached out to Monica for a little emergency marketing boost, which had thankfully paid off.

I glanced back at Wally and admitted, "I had help from a friend, so I can't take all the credit."

"Well, tell your friend thank you."

Warm feelings of accomplishment seeped inside me. Helping Wally with his play had never been on my radar, but it had kept me busy and bought me some more time in the city as I awaited an official job opportunity. But now that I was closing in on the end of the hectic week, all my efforts were beginning to pay off, and I was grateful for the opportunity. I affirmed his optimism by saying, "Let's hope that everything else goes smoothly, and the reviews from tonight come in strong in the morning. Then it should be smooth sailing for the next two weeks."

I waited for him to agree but instead his eyes darted past me as he got visually distracted by something. Then he greeted someone behind me with a casual nod. "Hey, what's up?"

The long pause that proceeded aided an increasing hollowness in the air, which suddenly ended with what felt like an arrow straight into my back. Someone was staring at me from behind. Then I heard the voice I had been avoiding for weeks say, "I don't know. Maybe you should tell me?" I instantly sat straight up like the back of my chair had shot out needles. *It was Fulton.*

It wasn't that I didn't want to see him because I did—my heart was madly pining for him—but I had absolutely no clue what I was supposed to say to him. No matter what I thought about, my trust issues would road block my heart with giant flashing signs saying, *Liar!* I had begged the heavens for my old life back—when I trusted him more than anyone—but then I remembered that the trust I used to hold had been naïve because it was based on lies. I knew I needed to forgive him, but it was too raw. *I needed time.* Unfortunately, Fulton was obviously not following the same timeline. With regret on my face, I slowly swiveled on my stool, turning to look at him. I cringed, waiting to see him go ballistic, but when I finally raised my eyes to greet his, I saw no anger— only devastation.

My cheeks warmed, and out of the corner of my eye, I saw Wally stand up, ready to speak. I didn't want him to make any excuses for me. I held up my hand to stop him and blurted out, "I can explain."

Staying silent, Fulton held up his phone, flashing the screen at me. I squinted to see what he had displayed; it looked like an email. I strained my neck to get a little closer and saw it was the marketing blast Monica had sent out. Then Fulton pointed to something in the email, which I didn't need to read. He was pointing to my name. I hadn't seen a final proof of the graphic because we had been in a hurry to get it sent, but I recalled Monica saying she added my name as co-director to add artistic appeal to the production. When I didn't say anything, Fulton looked at Wally and said, "Did you forget I was on your email list when you sent out an email bragging about what you two have been up to?"

"You can leave Wally out of this." I looked at Wally, who gave me one of those glances that can only be described as appreciative. Then I continued, "I know this looks weird. I guess, I don't know."

"You don't know?" He flashed his phone back at me and pointed to the ad. "You have no idea what this is about?"

"I do." Then I stole a sideways glance at Wally, who was looking more uncomfortable by the minute. He clearly didn't want to be in this awkward position. "I can explain. It's really not a big deal, and Wally shouldn't have to be in the middle of our drama." I lowered my voice and continued, "Let's go talk somewhere else." I motioned for Fulton to follow me, and then I walked forward with him right by my side. Once we were by ourselves, I explained, "I have a little room back here where we can talk in private."

"You have a room?" he asked. "You're supposed to be in Paris. How do you have a room here?"

My shoulder blades cinched with all levels of my consciousness feeling on-edge about everything that was happening with Fulton. However, I had a new realization—or at least one I hadn't admitted before—I was extremely embarrassed by my situation. A queasiness crept into my stomach, not from the guilt of not calling him, but of total humiliation. Even though he had been the person who had been by my side through some of the most embarrassing situations of my life, it was tremendous torture to let my guard down like this. The exposure I felt from him knowing more about my dad than I did was still hanging over me. I didn't think I could handle feeling more vulnerable. I had no idea how I was going to explain how I had been let go from my job, was unable to find a new job, was now practically homeless, and was crashing on Wally's hundred-year-old sofa.

So, without words, I opened the door to my room, flicked on the light and said, "I've been crashing here while I job search." I watched his jaw drop. When he didn't say anything, I added, "It's sort of a long story, but Gabby had to let me go. I got back to the city a couple weeks ago and was interviewing for jobs—none of which worked out. So, I was supposed to stay at my mom's." Then I gave up my last remaining fragments of dignity and shrugged, saying, "This was easier."

His eyes panned the sofa, still looking like it was recently time-warped from a black-and-white silent movie. Then he glanced at the surrounding stacked storage boxes covered in a thick film of dust that also lingered in the stale air that I'm sure he was choking on. He politely held back any smart comments about it. Not that Fulton ever said anything rude or overly sarcastic. I was more reflecting on how I would have reacted if the roles would have been reversed. I would have been crazy upset at him for not calling me. I hung my head low, waiting for him to come unglued, scream, and go crazy. However, he didn't, which sort of made my anxiety worse because now I had to *anticipate* being screamed at the way I used to have to dread my mom going crazy.

After way too long of silence while I shredded my lip with my teeth—terrified like the floor was going to open and swallow me into a pit of fire—I finally eased, telling myself Fulton *wasn't* my mom. He was normal and good at relationships. I almost fell backwards when the first words out of his mouth were: "I'm sorry."

Stunned in the weird reverse psychology he was playing on me, I said, "You're sorry. Why are you sorry?"

His eyes fled back to the floor, but I knew his sudden eye sweep wasn't an avoidance. I knew his avoidance stare. This was done of respect, with him wanting to give me space by not looking at me. "I—I think I overreacted," he said softly.

"You did?" I was astonished that he was taking the blame. "No, you didn't. I've been avoiding you."

He gave his head a shallow shake. "Not for that. Just—" He ran a hand through his hair, and if I hadn't known better, I would have said his hand looked a little shaky. It was more of a nervous thing, which was weird because he was never anxious around me. "The way I came down here and sort of assumed all these things."

"As you should have."

Fulton stepped away from the door, turning toward me. "Look, I didn't mean to invade your space. Like I said, I got that email and was confused and didn't really believe it. I didn't even know you were in town, and I was—"

"—hurt." I locked eyes with him for the first time since he had appeared in the lobby. I had expected him to make this conversation all about him, at which I would have been prepared to fight back with all these things I had been going through and why I needed to defend myself. His reaction didn't surprise me in that I knew he wasn't like that. My mom was like that, and for some reason my mind kept flashing back to fights with my mom. I pushed her memory out of the way and focused on Fulton. Sweet Fulton—he had always been the one to linger in the background, witnessing everything yet never judging. Out of all the qualities I adored about him—and there were many—his ability to support me while remaining neutral to the insanity was probably my favorite thing about him.

But relationships needed boundaries, and I had crossed a big one by blowing him off for weeks. Now I was exposed. I waited for him to open up about his feelings, but he wasn't giving me any of that. This was different than any other conversation that I had with him. It was evident in the way he shifted his shoulders toward the door when I asked him if he was hurt, but it was even more obvious in the way he crossed his arms in front of his chest that he was putting up a wall.

I should have apologized.

If I could go back, I would have apologized. Fulton was too good of a guy to not forgive me. It wasn't my pride that held me back because I didn't have any of that. It was my brokenness. My life had been shattered into such fine pieces that any decent wind could have camouflaged them amongst the dust. All my memories, my whole life, and my desire to have a healthy relationship had been demolished. Then another thought flashed like a yellow caution light, telling me Fulton had always been too good for me I was a fool for not seeing it sooner.

A wave of guilt washed up from my stomach when I looked at him standing there, still speechless. My eyes synchronized with his, and for a moment, I swear I saw a crossroads inside his eyes. One side was winding but gently leading forward, showing me all that could be. The other path was fast and narrow, wrapping up all that never was. Then, with a zapping, my mind refocused on his irises, still entwined with mine, and I was cemented. Like bricks layering among fresh mortar, sealing up a stone hedge around my heart, all my feelings closed in, and my heart had chosen a path.

I wished I had stayed speechless. I wished Fulton had given me more time. In this moment, I couldn't open my heart in the way he needed me to, and it wasn't fair to continue to childishly string him along. *He is a good guy,* I told myself. *No, he's a great guy.* I clenched my fists, squeezing my fingernails into my palms. *You're going to regret it.* If this was a ballet, the music would have stopped. *Don't do it,* I inwardly cried. I raised my face to meet his. I don't think I've ever felt more alive than I did in this moment; the deep heartache didn't cease for even a moment, reminding me that I was nothing more than a flawed human who could endure emotions. One look told me that I didn't need to say anything. He already knew all what I had been wrestling with. In a dangerous whisper that seemed to echo for days, he confirmed what I wanted to tell him. "You don't trust me, do you?"

I swallowed, wishing I could offer a rebuttal or at least beg that I would learn, and that I could rebuild it. *I couldn't.* It wasn't fair. It was just another notch in the tragedy of my spiraling life, and if this was a ballet, the lights would have blackened. But it wasn't theatre. It was my life.

Chapter Seventeen

That night, a bittersweet air enwrapped my life as I plunged forward, away from Fulton. Grateful for what we had, I felt a sweet relief that I wouldn't be at risk of getting hurt anymore. I was also filled with the success of our play but haunted with the reminder that I had no job offers. With the play officially launched, my time at the theatre had finally ended. I begrudgingly returned to my mom's condo.

It shouldn't have bothered me to stay there because I was alone since she was at treatment. However, after only a few days I found myself standing outside my mom's hospital room door. It was adorned with a welcome wreath that seemed to yell at me to "Go back, you fool!" Give me zombies or vampires or even aliens. I could easily handle any of them but having to make peace with my mom—mission impossible. Desperate and destitute, I knocked on the door. When no one replied, I let myself in. Even the hinges seemed to warn me one last time to run away as they wailed from their movement.

The lights were low, giving me the notion that she was still resting. I softly padded forward then winced as the haunted hinges wailed when I shut the door. Mom was sitting on her bed. No makeup painted her face, but she had more color in her skin tone than the last time I had seen her.

"Hi Mom," I said from my safe spot by the door.

"Hi," she replied in a neutral tone. She wasn't moaning, nor was she manic. I can handle neutral. I had thought about what I was going to say. I was tired of passive-aggressiveness and decided to get right into the reason why I came. Holding up the discharge papers I had in my hand, I said, "I met with your treatment coordinator, and he agreed to release you." Her eyes grazed the papers in my hand. Then I added, "I'm busting you out."

She looked at me suspiciously. "How?"

"I just signed you out." I didn't want to get into the details about how I had found some papers at the condo that showed my dad had named me her co-conservator to help Kim out once he was gone. The reasonable part of my brain wanted me to ignore her being in here because that was easiest for me, but my heart kept poking me, reminding me that she didn't do well in these types of places. It also didn't seem fair to me to stay at her home while she was locked up. I held up my dance bag that minutes before had all my belongings in it. I had dumped them on the sofa before I left this morning. "I can collect your things if you tell me which drawers you want me to look in."

She slid off the bed and reached her hand out for the bag. "I can do it." Her hand momentarily bumped mine, and I noticed how white her knuckles were. In fact, her whole body appeared frail. This place was aging her. I would never say that Montana had been good for her health because she had a crisis there too, but at least she had the faintest hues of pink in her cheeks. Here, she could almost be passed for dead with the right Halloween costume.

I let go of the bag when I felt her grip it. "Your treatment coordinator has to talk to you before you leave," I told her. "But he said we can stop in his office on our way out."

She made odd oral inventories of her things, as she combed through her possessions, naming them out loud when she packed them. Her inventory of them wasn't a normal checklist of things to grab but more of like an affirmation of an attachment, just like a child might double-check their favorite stuffed animals before going to sleep.

She packed, we met with her treatment coordinator to set up appointments with an outpatient program and we—no she—was finally free. I watched her face the entire time we were walking, wondering what it had to feel like to be able to know that you were going home after staying in a place like this. "Would you like to go for breakfast?" I asked after finally acknowledging my own hunger pains.

Her eyes were still glazed over the way they were when she was in treatment. In time she would be back to neutral, or worse—fuzzy unibrow.

I scanned the street, then said, "I'm not familiar with the area. Is there some place nearby that you know of that's good to eat?"

We had reached the car and both climbed in, shutting our doors in unison. I sat in silence for a moment because I wanted a plan before I started driving since I wasn't a super confident driver, especially in new towns. When she didn't offer any restaurants she liked, I pulled out my phone and started a search. "It looks like there is a diner down the street," I offered. "We could try that. Diners usually have a little bit of everything on the menu."

"No, don't go there. I'm not hungry." I could tell that she was thinking by the way she rolled her bottom lip under her teeth. I was getting hangrier by the minute because I had skipped breakfast, and I didn't understand what issue she would have with getting something to eat. My mom could never have a normal conversation or make a normal decision. I cranked the engine, making an executive decision to start driving in the direction of the diner. "Well, I'm super hungry. I'll start driving there," I said. "But if you know a better place, tell me where to turn." I pulled out of the parking lot onto the street, heading toward the restaurant.

"I don't want to go there."

"Is there somewhere else you like?" I gritted my teeth as I waited for her to answer me. Trying to get information out of my mom was like trying to get information out of a guilty toddler. In so many ways, my mom was forever childlike.

"I don't think so."

I slowed down because I could see my destination, and I started to scan for a parking spot. I was about to turn my wheel to pull in next to the sidewalk when she repeated loudly, "Don't go there."

"I asked you where you wanted to go, and you said nothing!" I screamed at her. A car behind me honked their horn, causing all my frustration to spiral into my foot. Since I wasn't able to park, I floored my gas pedal and sped forward. "What's the big deal? I'm hungry and thought it would be nice for us to share a meal together. Why can't you just go along with it? Are you crazy!" I screamed at her once I was down a block.

Gripping my wheel tightly, I now vowed that I wasn't going to pretend everything was normal by taking her out for breakfast. I pressed the accelerator down even further and rerouted my car toward the freeway. "We're going back to the condo," I announced and then I felt my shoulders relax back into the leather seat as I locked my eyes on the road ahead, grateful that I didn't have to look at my mom for the next nine miles.

My dad would have known what to do with her. I had no idea how to take care of a crazy person who hated me. It was insanity that I even felt like I had the obligation to try. *Dad*, I silently prayed, *you gotta help me.* I didn't get an answer from him but after a good minute of heavy silence, I turned my face back to my mom and said, "I don't know how to help you, but this isn't going to work. I know you can't go back to the hospital, but I'm lost."

I inwardly begged for an answer, but my prayers went unanswered, and one Tchaikovsky CD later, I pulled into her driveway. We hadn't spoken again, and I was left feeling terrified that I had made the wrong decision.

Chapter Eighteen

And like falling asleep into a bad nightmare where your whole world changes into a medieval ruin, I was living with my mom again. Nightmares didn't get any scarier than this. The first day was horrendous. She was constantly in my space, and I couldn't relax. I had to wait until she had retired upstairs behind her closed bedroom door, until I could finally let my guard down. Then I wasted no time and pulled out my phone, searching for a job out of pure desperation to get out of here. I was soon frustrated because all the jobs I was interested in already had tons of applicants.

I glossed over one entry-level designer position for a new line of woman's shoes and the first thing the application asked for was my objective. I wrinkled my nose and said, "To not have to live with my mom." Although I knew that wasn't what they were looking for, the whole task of getting a job seemed so daunting. I was ahead of most kids my age, having already been working for over a year, but I was too far behind other degreed professionals who were competing for the same type of jobs. I wasn't much for math, but it seemed like the amount of time needed to apply for each job was a waste of time when I could be working.

I set my phone down and reached over the arm of the couch, pulling out my sketchbook that had been tucked into the side pocket of my dance bag. Opening the front cover, I let my eyes scan the first page until I found adequate white space. In my best penmanship, I wrote:

Objective: Stop searching. Create.

That was it. That was my mission. It had to be.

Tapping my fingers on my sketchpad, my mind drifted from the vintage dresses I had studied all the way to the high-end couture fashion I helped Gabby sell in her store. None of that struck me as something I needed to create. I put my pen to my pad and drew one line with a slight curve. I had never studied drawing, but I had found over the last year that I was a natural at it because I loved lines. That was left over from my ballet days as there was a great beauty in something as simple as a perfect curve, and there was strength in a straight line.

I loved how in ballet each movement was choreographed so that when they were threaded together you had a movement that was graceful and cohesive with the next movement. I also loved how that had a transferability to drawing fashion. You needed great lines that flowed into the next. I looked down at my pad and realized I had drawn a ballerina in first position, but the part of the picture that pulled me in was that I had drawn a pretty fantastic leotard on her. With a laser focus, I took my pencil and began to shade in a pattern for texture. Then I pulled the picture back and studied it. It was daring me to do something *different*.

"Hmm," I thought out loud. The thing with leotards was that they are meant to be the same, so that when you were in class all the dancers moved together, and it was easy to look at. "But what if there was a way to make a leotard personalized without it being seen?" I asked myself. Something to give a dancer a little bit of confidence and be able to share her personality. Some people have lightbulb moments, but this was different. In a quick twist of thought pattern, I knew exactly what I was going to create.

With a renewed zeal, I tore through the first few pages of my sketchpad, discarding anything that was going to cloud up my canvas for my creation. When I was satisfied that my notebook had been purged of any stale ideas, I drew it: a perfectly simple pink leotard that was plain and unremarkable to the average eye. I smirked as I penciled in the secret, right above the right leg opening seam. In the same color pink, I wrote in cursive, *"Fierce."*

It was a word that Fulton had once used to describe the way I danced, and I had let it saturate as not only one of the best compliments I had ever received but also as a personal motto. I would embroider the word so small that no one would ever see it, especially once the dancer's skirt was laid over the top of it, but it was a detail that I knew would have given me courage. I instantly saw a personalized product line where dancers could order whatever word they wanted to give them motivation. It Could work. Dancing was like any other professional sport that required devoted hard work. It often went unnoticed—sometimes forever—and dancers used a lot of things to help motivate them. This was an idea that was niche, just like when I sewed those silly butt patches on jeans, but it wasn't as cheesy.

Then, like a red-carpet unrolling, I saw my pitch, as my dad would call it. I was going to use my dance background to design clothing for dancers. They would sell because my clothes were going to be designed by a dancer who knew the intensity of the sport and the required endurance and comfort. I covered my mouth with my hands and tried not to scream. It seemed so easy. My dad had always said, "When you start a business, don't reach." He said that was how people got into trouble. They tried to dabble in things they didn't know because they saw the opportunity, and it was often more exciting than the things they already knew. But for me, this was perfect. I wasn't reaching. I knew dance. I knew design. I was blending.

I didn't care what time it was in Paris; I grabbed my phone to tell Gabby. She would support me and guide me, but before I could text, my thoughts were interrupted by an unread text. My brow lifted when I read who it was from.

Wally: *Hey Abs, I know this is sort of random, but can you give me a call when you get this?*

I let my fingers play with the edge of my phone while I re-read his request. I wondered what was up, but before my imagination played horrid scenarios, I pressed call on his name.

"Hey," he answered.

"Is it too late?"

"No, not at all. I own a theatre. Therefore, I'm always awake."

"Oh no." I giggled because I could hear a story coming from his comment. "What's going on now?"

"Oh, the usual. I'm still doing overnight cleaning, so I'll be up for another few hours."

"Ah." I could almost feel his stress coming from the phone. "Hopefully you can hire someone soon."

"I do have a plan," he declared with enthusiasm. "But I have to work out some other stuff first."

"That could be good."

"It is. But I know you don't want to hear about my cleaning. There's a reason I wanted you to call. I have something I want to talk to you about."

"Okay."

"I was hoping I could get you to come down here so we can talk in person. Would that be an option?"

My mind instantly added up the cost of a train ticket, and it made me bite my lip. I was broke. I much preferred he tell me what he wanted to say over the phone. "Is everything okay?" I asked, trying to field a little detail.

"Yeah," he rushed to confirm. "Everything is great. It's nothing bad. I know this is vague but I'm hoping you can trust me that I'm not wasting your time." I didn't have anything else to do so I didn't mind the idea of taking a short trip to visit him, but I honestly had no idea how I was going to pay for it. "Abs," he said, interjecting my thoughts, "please. You won't regret it. We are actually running the last night of our play Saturday. If you want to come to see how the show has evolved, I think you'll be pleased."

I was stunned with curiosity at this point. Before I could talk myself out of it, I said, "Okay, I'll do my best to come up this weekend."

"Good. You know where to find me when you get here."

"Yes, I do," I said, now aware that I was going to have to ask my mom for money. That made me ponder robbing a gas station instead, which then made me giggle because I knew my own moral code would never let me entertain an idea like that. I swallowed and said, "I'll get ahold of you when I'm there."

"Okay. See you this weekend."

I ended the call and set my phone on the floor next to the couch. I immediately lay down on my back to shut my eyes but instead of sleeping I stared at the ceiling, rehearsing how I was going to ask my mom for a loan. No matter what I said, it was going to be a hard sell. Part of me also didn't want to complicate our relationship more by making myself financially dependent on her. I smiled to the ceiling when I realized that my dad must have foreshadowed that about me when he pushed me hard to learn to work. I had been through a ton of stuff in the last year, but I wasn't afraid to work. Working for my money would be a better option than asking for a loan, and since I couldn't get a real job, that meant I was going to have to hustle in a different way.

Giving into my insomnia, I sat up and decided now was just as good a time as any to get ahead on my idea. I pulled out my notebook again and started to make a list of all the things I would need and the resources I already had. This late-night planning reminded me of how Gabby was always pulling all-nighters to get ahead. Then I remembered that she was on Paris time. Without more thought about it, I grabbed my phone and called her.

"Hey, Abs," she greeted me.

"Hi, is this a bad time?"

"No, not at all. I'm going over some spreadsheets that my tax person sent me. What about you?"

"I'm super stressed out and was hoping you could give me advice."

"Oh," her voice softened. "What's going on?"

"Well, as you know, my job search is not going well."

"Don't give up."

"I'm not. I'm sort of playing with a plan B."

"That's always good. It'll give you something to keep your mind busy. So, what's plan B?"

"I'm thinking of designing my own line of clothing for dancers. Sort of with the pitch 'Made by a Dancer for Dancers.' And I think I can make it work and all, but the problem is that I need money. That part I don't understand. How do I get money to do this?"

"That's a great question. Different people do different things. Sometimes people will work full time while they invest in a side business. Other times people will take out a business loan or get investors. You have a few options, so you don't need to decide overnight."

"That's the problem, though. I do need to decide overnight because I need money now. I'm out."

I heard her sigh on the other end of the phone. "I can't believe your dad didn't set up any sort of allowance for you once he passed at least to help with the transition."

"Maybe he did." I could feel my shoulders pinch together. "But he never said anything and the only way for me to pursue it at this point would be to ask my mom and we are in such a weird place right now that I can't see her giving me anything but the flash of a fuzzy unibrow."

I could hear Gabby let out a half-laugh like she thought I was joking but then she stifled it when she gathered that I was dead serious. "I'm sorry you have to go through this, but you might be one of those people who has to go out and get a waitressing job or something to start making money to pay bills. Then you can work on your clothing line on the side."

I wasn't opposed to a part-time job, but I knew it wasn't going to be fast enough. I needed money by Friday. I also knew that Gabby wasn't practical when it came to business. She was a risk-taker, so I pressed her. "What would you do?"

"Me?" I heard a light rebellious groan escape from her mouth, like she was trying to resist telling me. "I'm different, Abs. Don't use me as an example."

"Let me decide that. Tell me what you did to get started."

"I'd starve in order to live my dream."

"I know. That's why I called you."

"I maxed out credit cards and bank loans and anything I could get my hands on, but I would never recommend that for you."

"What would you recommend to me then?"

"Okay, let's talk this through. You need money now. You have an idea. You are going to design dance clothes, right?"

"Yes."

"Do you have a sample?"

"No, I have a sketch."

"Do you have any money or a credit card?"

"I have a credit card that my dad gave me for emergencies, but he obviously isn't going to pay for it now."

"Right . . . but you could pay for it."

"I could," I answered slowly, trying to see where she was going since she had just told me not to use a bunch of credit.

"So, use the credit card to get a sample of the clothes you have in the sketch. You can make it yourself or you can call my seamstress to help you. You'll have to pay her for fabric and her time, but I've always found she is worth the expense. Then take that sample and do a presale."

"What's that?"

"You basically don't have any product because you don't have the money, but if you sell the product before you make it, you will have the money first, so you can buy the materials. You can make people pay like fifty percent of the total price. Giving them a discount on the total price encourages them to buy it now instead of waiting until you have inventory. Then you will build your inventory as you sell the product. Make sense?"

"Sort of. But who am I going to sell it to on such short notice?"

"It's dance clothes, right?"

"Well, right now it's just a leotard, but yeah."

"Then go to dancers. You know where to find them."

"That's it? That's all I need to do to start this line?"

"In your situation, that's what I would do. I would start slow and sell as you go while growing. It's not going to be a lot of money right away, but it'll put you on my noodles and caffeine diet." She offered a light chuckle, and I knew she was trying her best to help me. It wasn't exactly the news I wanted to hear but it was something. My dad had always said, "A mediocre plan is better than no plan." So, I accepted her advice as a challenge and said, "Okay, I can do this. Thank you."

"No problem."

"I'll let you go so I can work on this sample."

"Good luck."

I ended my call and pulled out my sketch book, getting straight to work. As I prepared to send my sketch off, I swallowed. This was getting real.

Chapter Nineteen

When Friday arrived, I took the first train into the city to pick up my sample from Gabby's seamstress. To anyone else, it wasn't anything more than a leotard. To me, it was my ticket to living my life as a functioning adult. I double-checked the seams to make sure they were reinforced the way I had instructed. I had chosen a thicker fabric with support, because in all my years of dance, I always struggled with leotards that were too thin and unforgiving. I also hated leotards that had any sheen to them. I felt like once they got under the stage lights, the weird reflection helped to wash out my complexion.

Excitement built in my gut when I slipped the garment on and did a few stretches to make sure the fabric moved with me. I was going to move forward with this as my first design, and it was launching in less than an hour. I unfolded the matching leg warmers that I had ordered on a whim, and I was glad I included them as an upgrade. It completed the look and functioned well for keeping me warm.

"It's not a perfect plan," I repeated to myself again as I had done over and over the last couple of days, "but it's a plan." I eagerly paid for my design with my credit card and then wrapped my trench coat over my leotard and belted my coat. "I'm doing this." I pep-talked myself as I headed to my old dance studio where I had already made an appointment with my old dance instructor to show them my leotard. They were eager to hear about my idea, agreeing to let me set up a vendor table in the hall.

thought I would be nostalgic as I pulled the handle on the glass door to the dance studio, but I was oddly calm as I breezed right through the halls. I knew from my dad's testimonies that the best way to sell is to offer something that solved a problem, and the best people to sell to are people you have established trust with. My smile grew when I saw familiar faces, and many of them remembered me too. I took my place, standing in the hallway modeling my leotard and hoped for the best.

I stayed until the last class was over and the door was locked, then counted my pre-orders. It wasn't a homerun by any means. Most of the people had passed on them, saying that they'd wait until they could order online. However, I ended up with enough orders to pay for what I had charged on my credit card for the weekend, and that alone brought relief in my chest. I knew from working with Gabby that fashion was a hard business, so I told myself I had won today. Nothing was perfect. Everything had been rushed, but it came together.

I took a few moments to look at my reflection in the full mirror. I was wearing a leotard and leg warmers for the first time in years, but it didn't feel like it had been that long ago that I wore these clothes daily. I still had a ballet-slipper-sized hole somewhere in my heart, and I missed dancing. It wasn't from a place of vanity or need for attention either. It was an expression that had become like a sixth sense to me.

As much as I heard the empty barre calling my name, I didn't have time. I took a few minutes to call my seamstress to place my orders. When I was satisfied with the arrangement we verbally made over the phone, I changed back into my street clothes and headed to the theatre to meet Wally. I had tried my hardest to get there in time to see the show, but it was well into the second half when I walked through the doors. Wally was hunched over his computer in the ticket office, and he sat up straight when he saw me walk in. "Hey," he called out to me.

I walked up to the ticket office window, feeling uneasy. He closed his laptop and tucked it under his arm when he stood. Motioning to the door behind him, he said, "Come on back to the office." While he waited for me, he added, "Or did you want to sit in and watch the show?"

I shrugged, dismissing his invitation. "It's okay. I wanted to see it, but it has to be ending soon."

"That's what I thought." He opened the back door where I saw his dad, Henry, sitting at a small conference table.

Henry lifted his chin and greeted me. "Miss Purple."

I smirked at his cheesy nickname. "How are you?"

"Better now that you are here." Then he winked at me, the way old guys in nursing homes wink at the young nurses. "You can have a chair. Can I get you something from concessions for a snack? Or a soft drink, maybe?"

"I'm good," I said, taking a seat. I was totally taken back seeing Wally's dad as Wally hadn't given me any clues to what this meeting was even about. I kept my eyes glued to Wally, who closed the door behind us, the formality of his actions making me nervous.

Wally sat next to his dad and placed his laptop to rest in front of him. "I suppose you want to know what this is all about."

I sat on the edge of my seat, leaning forward. "Yeah, I'm sort of dying to know."

"Well, it's nothing bad," he started with, "so you can put your mind at ease."

"Okay."

"I had an idea a couple of days ago, and I talked to my dad." He motioned to Henry. "He thought my idea was great, so we thought we'd throw it at you to see what you thought. If you don't mind?" He looked at me like he was requesting permission to continue. I yielded with a nod, and he continued. "I vented to you before about how the theatre business was struggling, which is why I was exploring these plays. This Christmas play was an experiment, and even with throwing everything together last minute, we ended up having a phenomenal turnout. Most of the shows sold out, which was probably because they were free, but the reviews were surprisingly excellent."

I leaned forward and exclaimed, "That's fantastic."

"Yeah, people didn't have any complaints but then again, it was a free show. What are people going to complain about? Everything in the city's so expensive, and people expressed their appreciation for having a free family event. We made a killing on concessions because people were happy to support us that way."

"That's great." I bobbed my head with enthusiasm.

"It is great, but it was a *ton* of work. I barely slept more than a couple hours a night. I'd like to continue to offer these shows, especially during the days when the theatre would be sitting empty anyway, but I can't continue at this pace. I finally hired a cleaning person, since we have money to do that now. So going forward I'll have help with that at least."

"That'll be nice."

"It is. But you don't need to be bored with all those details. I wanted you to be able to sit down with my dad and talk about this idea I have."

He looked at his dad who picked up the conversation. "The show Wally wrote and put on was a huge success, mostly because of the non-existent overhead. I know that you stepped in to help him with some of the rrangements with the costumes and the dancers. We appreciate that for two reasons. One, we had many comments about how lovely the dancers were. Two, having a partnership with that dance company opened us up to a newer clientele. It's been fantastic."

My lips easily turned up at Henry. "I'm glad. I knew those girls would put on a great show."

"We also saw huge success because of the email marketing blasts you coordinated through your marketing contact." He looked at Wally. "What was her name?"

"Monica," Wally replied. Then he expanded on Henry's comment. "I actually reached out to Monica again after you did, and she did a lot of follow-up blasts that were relatively inexpensive. We were able to track how many of those emails converted to ticket sales, and it was a huge success. She knew exactly how to set up those emails to make people one-click. It was like magic."

Contentment swelled inside my heart while I listened to him brag about Monica, especially since she had been my dad's intern. My dad had taught her most of his tricks. In a weird way, I was able to see my dad's hand in this. "Monica is the best," I replied.

"I can't say enough good things about her or the other choices you suggested. This little play is like a gold mine for easy money," Henry said, locking eyes with me. "That brings us to why you're here. We would like to keep rolling with seasonal plays to keep people in the door. You did a great job with the tips you gave Wally, and you have extensive performing experience. I know you have your own career goals, and I totally understand that is your priority, but Wally mentioned something about how your job search wasn't going well. So we talked about it, and I thought we would throw it out there. We'd love to bring you on board to help Wally co-produce these shows." He paused, waiting for my response.

My jaw dropped as this was the last thing I had expected Wally to ever talk to me about. My gaze bounced back to Wally, his eyes sparkling with excitement. When I looked back at Henry, I knew he was sincere. I was getting a job offer! It wasn't at all even close to what I had envisioned myself doing, but it was a place for me to be able to utilize all my past work experience with ample room to grow. Even though I had already planned to create my dance clothing line, I knew that it would take time before it would be lucrative. I didn't need to ask questions. I couldn't have found a more trustworthy business partner. I stuck out my hand to offer a handshake to Henry and firmly stated, "Deal."

He chuckled when he took my hand and shook it. "I love your style. No fretting. Just business."

"I know we'll have to work out details as we move forward, but I also know that this is one of the few things that has made sense to me in a while. I would hate myself for not jumping in." Then my eyes skirted back to Wally, and I said, "Thank you so much for taking this risk on me. I promise I won't disappoint you."

"We know you'll do well," Wally said. "And since it's a new position, you're free to take it and run with it. We can tailor it to fit what you enjoy, and we will keep our conversation ongoing about how things are working or not working."

"It's going to be amazing. I'm excited," I said with zeal.

"Good," Wally said. "I guess the only thing we need to make it official is to determine a start date. I'm guessing you'll need time to move, but we can be flexible."

Apprehension grew in my throat for the first time in the conversation. I had been so relieved to finally have a job offer that it hadn't dawned on me that there was a huge logistical boulder barreling down on my happiness. Wally must have read my anxiety because without waiting for me to embarrass myself by having to explain my whole situation, he looked at his dad and said, "New York housing is a mess. I would hate for her to rush into an apartment she doesn't love because it's all she can find, and she needs to start work. Don't you think she could crash in Nana's room so she can take her time to find the right place?"

If there ever was a doubt in my life who my true friends were, it wasn't at this moment. I felt immense gratitude that Wally was not only going to bat with his dad to hire me, but that he was doing his best to save me the humiliation of trying to explain that I was poor. I was so touched by how he defended me, tears started to well in my eyes. I mouthed, "Thank you," to Wally from across the table. He winked back at me without his dad seeing.

Henry agreed by saying, "Yeah, I think that would be fine if she wants to stay here."

I tried to hide my super giddy grin because I didn't want to seem childish, but inside, I was doing every twirl combo I could think of. A gregarious grin to escaped my lips when I said, "That would be nice. Then I can start right away and won't be stressed about housing."

"Perfect," Henry said, and he pulled out his keyring. The thing resembled a janitor's packed ring. Without confusion, he went to a small gold key and threaded it off his ring. Handing it over to me, he said, "This was Nana's copy. Consider it yours."

I took the key and looked at it like it was a treasured jewel. "Thank you."

"You'll need an office anyway. That's probably the best place to put you since it's backstage and right by where all your work will be." Then he stood up and acknowledged us both once more. "It's hard to be a leader in this industry, and you guys made a great team. I'm excited to see what comes next. Let's shoot for a Valentine's Day production to launch at the beginning of February."

"That will be perfect," I said.

"Great," Henry said in a definitive tone, ending the meeting. "I hate to run, but it's the playoffs, and I have a ball game to watch." Then he added, "If you work hard when you are young like you are, then when you get to be my age, recreation can be more important than work."

I wasn't worried about my decision to join Wally on his project because I trusted Wally. Plus, it was the only offer I had. Unless

I wanted to flip burgers, I would be stupid to turn this offer down. However, there was a tiny bit of apprehension sitting in my stomach, worrying about if I would be enough. I worried that maybe this first play was a fluke, and that they were giving me too much credit for things that were beyond my control. Maybe I wouldn't be a huge asset going forward, but when Henry spoke to me about life, his advice went straight to my heart. He was giving me fatherly advice the way my dad used to.

Knowing that God puts people in your life for a reason, I knew I'd learn business from Henry. Even more than that, I knew he was going to be one of those timeless father figures full of wisdom that I desperately needed for this season of my life. I dropped my eyes, overwhelmed at how clearly I saw my path now. I couldn't have planned it better than it was working out. Henry had left the room now, allowing Wally to speak candidly to me. He wasted no time before breaking into a huge boyish grin. "You know I have no idea what I'm doing, so you are going to have to be able to steer this ship around the iceberg."

I laughed and said, "If we crash, we'll go down together."

"Good. I'm glad you accepted this position." He softened his voice and said, "I think it's the perfect position for you, but to be honest, I've been worried about you."

I blinked when I realized where he was bringing this conversation, but I trusted that he wouldn't pry too much. "I'll be okay," I affirmed. "It's been crazy, but I think I'm on track. But really—" I paused while I waited for him to catch my eyes with his. "Thank you for this opportunity. I totally understand it's not just about some silly plays. This is your family's legacy, and I would never take that lightly."

It was his turn to be quiet. Then his eyes bounced back up to me with a renewed eagerness. "I forgot that someone was here waiting for you."

"Me?"

"A lady showed up asking about you. I thought it was sort of a coincidence, but you were on your way. She said she was going to stay to watch the show and would check after it was over to see if you were here."

"Did she say her name?"

"I don't think I asked. Sorry."

"It's okay." My mind instantly went to Gabby. She was one of the only people who I had kept in touch with over this last month. Even though she was busy, I knew she had the heart to take the time to surprise me to support me. I stood up and walked toward the door. "I bet I know exactly who it is."

Chapter Twenty

I missed Gabby so much, I sprinted through the door, landing amongst hordes of people all walking toward the exit. My eyes raced through the crowd, sifting through the faces as I looked for Gabby's petite frame. I was so dialed in on finding that one silhouette that I didn't notice when someone approached me and tried to get my attention. As I walked right past her, she managed to reach back her arm and gently squeeze my wrist to stop m. I whipped around, excited to see Gabby, but Gabby wasn't there—it was Becky.

Becky and I had been inseparable our entire childhood, but after I moved to Montana, our friendship sadly fizzled out. However, seeing her here tonight felt like I was having a reunion with a long-lost sibling. I covered my mouth and suppressed a girly squeal that I didn't even know I was capable of doing anymore, and I hugged her. "Becky!"

She hugged me back. "Amazing show you worked on."

I shook off her compliment. "Oh, it's not really my work. My friend wrote it. I came in at the end of the project."

"I'm sure you're being modest." Becky beamed at me. "I got an email that said you were the talent director for this show, and I know we haven't talked much but I had to see you."

"I missed you too," I said lightly. Her presence felt warm and supportive. Before I had a chance to continue my comment, she stunned me by breaking out into quiet tears. "What's wrong?" I asked, my concern piqued. She rubbed her cheek with the back of her hand to wipe her tears, but they were quickly replaced with more wet drops. "It's okay." I touched her arm to console her.

Refusing my condolence with a fast shake of her head, she said, "No, I'm sorry. I'm sorry about your dad . . ."

That word, *dad*, instantly and always got hinged in my throat, but tonight was my happy night. I couldn't be sad, so I cut her. "It's okay."

She rambled on, "I'm sorry about your mom."

"You know about my mom?" I could have slammed my palm on my forehead. Of course, she knew about my mom because her mom was best friends with my mom. Becky had always known things about my life that only a sister should know, even though I never had the guts to admit it to her.

Becky didn't pause for a breath as she continued to apologize. With a muffled tear-filled voice, she said something I couldn't decipher. "I'm sorry," she sniffed, "about the dress."

In my almost twenty years of knowing her, there was still only one dress she would cry about. An alarm buzzed in my brain, echoing her words. I didn't need to ask. I already knew she had been involved in a prank to ruin Gabby's fashion week dress to get me in trouble. I had suspected that Tina had chopped up my dress, and Becky had kept the secret. Becky's eyes rained out remorse, and through her sobs, she said, "It was me! I cut your dress!"

Her sobs were so hard, I extended my arms, offering a hug. She immediately walked forward to receive it. That dress drama felt like another lifetime ago, but I recalled how that stunt had actually worked out in my favor, and frankly I was over it. "It's okay," I said. "I'm not mad."

She lifted her face, and red blotches now stained the tops of her cheeks. She took another deep breath, and then she asked, "How come you're not mad?"

I lifted a shoulder. "It worked out."

She sniffed one last time. "I thought you hated me."

"No, I didn't hate you. I just felt like we were in two different places in life. You were still in high school . . . and I was trying to learn how to be an adult."

"That's how I felt too, but I was jealous of you."

"Jealous of me?" A mirage flowed through my head filled with everything from living in the sticks, to having to survive my mom, to losing my dad. Each of my memories seemed to parallel with something in her life. I had been banished to a tiny home while she thrived in a Park Avenue penthouse. I had a crazy mom while her mom was literally the most respected real estate agent in the tri-state area. She graduated from an elite private school while I got an online certificate. The mirage of images went on and on. "Why would you be jealous of me?"

"You got this great job working with a famous designer and had this adult life while I was still in high school, living with my parents. I felt like you looked down on me."

I rested my teeth on my top lip as I recalled feeling that I had grown beyond Tina and Becky. I hadn't known they felt it too, but all of that didn't matter anymore. Even though our lives didn't synchronize last year, I had a feeling it would be better now. "It's okay," I said. "Let's just put all that behind us." I opened my arms wide for another hug. "Friends?"

"Friends," she affirmed and hugged me one more time. My heart had a feeling that can only be described as something akin to a homecoming, but I wasn't ready to be done talking to her. Then I remembered I was still clenching Nana's dressing room key. I held it out for her to see, saying, "We have so much catching up to do, but let's not stand in the middle of the hall. Would you like to see my office?"

Her smile brightened. "Of course." Our steps synchronized the way they used to when we would walk through the halls of school together. Tonight, we were moving forward in our friendship, and it felt right.

Chapter Twenty-One

It was hours past dark, and Wally had long since locked up the theatre and went home by the time I had finally sent off Becky in a cab. As I wove back through the theatre aisles on my way to my office, my cheeks ached from grinning. The few times I had spoken with Becky over the last years, we had been in two different seasons of life, making it impossible to connect. However, now that she was out of high school and attending college, our personalities once again complemented each other. Reconnecting with Becky wasn't something that I would have ever sought after, but after spending the last several hours laughing and sharing our life's updates, I could tell I needed her in my life.

I breezed up the side stage steps, but a light tapping hit the middle of my back. My feet halted. Slowly, I pivoted my neck and confirmed that I was alone. Not seeing anything out of the ordinary, I excused it as a lack of sleep and continued to climb the last couple of steps. Then I got another tap. I didn't want to look again, because I was seriously getting creeped out. I did an insanely fast glance over my shoulder before telling myself I was being paranoid. My imagination flashed to the upstairs wall, displaying photos of the entertainers who had performed here. A good portion of the photos were black and white and most of those people were long since dead. The hairs on my arm stood when I considered if *maybe* one of them were still here.

No, that couldn't be. I'm seriously overtired.

I quickly climbed the last step, and the tapping came again. This time it was on the top of my head, and I shrieked! A white kernel of popcorn bounced on the floor by my feet. Relief cleansed my veins, and I pivoted on my heel on the hunt for Wally.

I yelled at the little window in the projector room. "Okay, you got me! I was super scared." I chuckled, waiting for Wally to poke his curly haired clown head through the projector door so he could laugh at me. The face I saw was more familiar than Wally's—it was Fulton.

Our eyes locked, and even with the distance between us, I still felt a connection to him which instantly sent a warm rush to my face. "Hey."

"Hey, you," he called. "Stay right there. I'll come down."

My feet planted to the top step and a moment later, he jogged over to me. In a directness that he was known for, he asked, "Can we talk?"

Feeling trapped, I couldn't deny that something was happening in my heart as it thumped against my ribs. "Sure," I said, sitting down on the step. "So, did Wally show you how to throw popcorn at me?"

He effortlessly boosted himself up onto the stage next to me. "He confessed about the two of you throwing popcorn at me, if that's what you're asking."

I innocently held my hand on my chest. "What?"

His eyes twinkled softly in a way that made my gut uneasy. "I actually think it was pretty cute."

"I have no idea what you are talking about," I said, pleading my innocence. I felt good being playful with Fulton, but then he leaned closer, and his eyes moved across my face, sending a wave of insecurity down my body. *I missed him so much.*

"Wally called me to get my opinion about your job offer. I had to fill him in with what was going on with us. He said he didn't know. Then he mentioned you were on your way up tonight. So . . ."

"Oh." I steeled my face into a neutral position.

"I was planning on surprising you, but Becky . . ." He paused, flashing his perfect teeth. "She beat me to you, so I've literally been stuck up there where it's smolderingly close to the furnace room for the last three hours."

"That's funny." I giggled at his ambition, feeling half bad because Becky and I had taken our sweet time.

"To you." His laughter was just as strong as mine. "How is she?"

"Good." I nodded my head slowly, recalling how great it was to see her again. "She is working for her mom. Actually, her mom is letting her stay in one of their company apartments, and she has an extra bedroom that she invited me to rent."

"Really?" He quirked a brow, leaning closer like he was genuinely interested in the details of my life. It stung in a way that reminded me of the friendship we had.

"Yeah, and it couldn't be more perfect timing. Wally's dad said I could stay here—" I motioned toward my office "—but I don't feel comfortable taking so much from them. Our arrangement will feel more professional if I get my own place. So, I'm glad something came up so quickly.".

"I think you and Becky will be great roommates." When he looked at me, he gave me a heated gaze that warned the light-hearted part of our conversation was over. I licked my lips, expecting him to lead with an apology again, even though I didn't think he owed me another apology. But that didn't happen. "I saw Candace again."

What! I managed to not flinch. *Was he trying to make me jealous?* "Okay . . ."

"I was upset by how you expected me to be perfect, while you definitely forgot about your mistakes pretty fast," he rambled with urgency. "Remember how you used to be mean to me all the time?" His eyes narrowed, and it gave me a bad taste in my mouth. My lips parted but I couldn't speak. He didn't have a problem venting, and he apparently had a lot to get off his chest. "I was infuriated that you only gave me one shot after everything I forgave you for. She reached out to me and asked if I wanted to get together. I'm not perfect, so I went to see her. But the crazy thing was I just thought about you the whole time, which made me more upset at you." He paused and I fought like crazy to avoid looking at him, but his superior eye-trapping skills defeated my weak avoidance. "We need to fix this."

"Way to play hard to get," I commented with a soft sarcasm in my voice.

"I don't play games," he said gently. "You know that."

I chewed the side of my cheek while I tried to think of an excuse as to why it wasn't a good idea to fix us. When I looked up at him, I noticed the back of his hairline was beaded in sweat from sitting in that hot room, waiting for me all night long—a symbol of fierce loyalty. But that didn't make me happier, because the obsessive part of my brain reminded me that it was the same loyalty that drove him to cover up lies for my dad. I was right back where I always got stuck. I knew he was loyal. That wasn't my issue. My issue was with the lies. "It's too hard," I finally admitted.

"No." He shook his head empathically and his voice conveyed a sternness. "You just buried the one person who took care of you your whole life, and he was arguably the only person you ever felt loved by. Now you're pushing me away. I'm not dumb. I've known you your whole life, and you don't let people in. Ever. The only friends you had in school were mean ones. You quickly became a workaholic to avoid any chances of having to be social and make new friends. You're afraid of our relationship because love scares you, and you are using this for a reason to push me away."

My heart did an ungraceful belly flop when he said the word *love*. It wasn't a word Fulton, and I used, but harder than that, it wasn't a word I had ever really heard even from my parents. I didn't like being vulnerable. My eyes fled to my feet while preparing the most honest words I had ever admitted to him. "I don't know how to love anyone."

"That's not true," he picked up perfectly on cue like I knew he would.

But before he could tell me all the things he thought he understood about me, I spoke over him. "It's true. I mean, I can feel strongly about things, but when it comes to people, I have this constant fear that disables my ability to feel love." I raised my eyes to meet his. "The more I get close to someone, the more I feel afraid."

Fulton furloughed his brow and took a defensive tone, "It can be scary, but it's worth—"

I cut him off. "No, it's not scary. It's like fire ice embalms my veins, restricting flow to my vital organs, and I get suffocated from the inside." I could tell I confused him with my graphic explanation, because his forehead was stacked with lines. His lips parted like he was going to respond. I couldn't say this much without explaining the rest, so I quickly continued. "When I was little, my dad took me to a fair—just the two of us—and he won me a pet goldfish. I was like seven years old, and I thought it was the most beautiful thing ever—the way she swam so majestically like a dance of her own—and I named her after my favorite ballerina." My voice quickened, "Then the next week, I had a dance recital, but my parents didn't come because my mom had issues. No one even told me they couldn't make it. I stood on the stage next to all the other girls. Their families came up with bouquets of flowers, hugging them. I kept straining my neck, waiting to see my dad with something special for me, but no one came.

I had to take the bus home by myself and wait on the front steps until my dad got home. I didn't even have a stupid key to the house. When I got inside, I took my fish out of the water and watched her wiggle for air. My dad saw me and yelled for me to put her back in the water, but I squeezed her until she didn't move anymore. Then my dad pried my hand open, and we both saw the fish had died. When I didn't get upset, my dad freaked out and took me to a psychiatrist. The shrink said that a normal kid would cry when their pet fish died. Since I showed no emotion, he diagnosed me with some stupid attachment disorder and said I didn't know how to love. So, like, it's a real thing. I don't know how. Even a doctor said it." I licked my lips, satisfied with my confession but still a little breathless.

When I finally had the bravery to meet his eyes, I expected him to be horrified that I murdered my fish, but instead of being wide-eyed, his irises were soft with empathy. He reached out, touching me for the first time, and a wave of tingles shot through my arm when he squeezed my hand. "I knew about Fonteyn."

"You did?" I asked in a voice barely above a whisper.

"Just because some stupid doctor said that to you when you were seven doesn't mean you don't know how to love."

"What does it mean, then?"

He shrugged like he was just as lost as I was. "It means . . . that you were a kid who was deeply wounded for like the millionth time by your parents, and you built Fort Knox around your heart because of it all. I get it, and I understand why. So, you might be a little neurotic about this stuff, and you might need more time to trust me, but so what?" He squeezed my hand, and my heart pined back. "You're worth it."

"I don't understand how you can be so sure." I was still trying to give him a way out.

He lowered his eyes. "It's like a Super Nova sort of thing."

"Huh?" My brows lifted at his ever-geeky science knowledge that he always seemed to bring up at the most inappropriate times.

Leaning closer to me, I got a hint of his aftershave, and it instantly reminded me that his scent was one of longing. Lucky for me, Fulton had entered story mode, and I didn't have to pretend that I was struggling with being this close to him. "There's a law of physics that says, for every action, you get an equal reaction. It's having to do with the energy released. A Supernova is one of creations rarest things, and it happens when a star runs out of fuel. There is a pressure release, and to balance the change in pressure with the star's gravity, an implosion happens, and then that causes waves that bounce back out and create another explosion."

"I don't get it," I said dryly.

"It's extreme. It's probably the largest known balance of energy in the galaxy. It's violent, yet the dust that it leaves behind is *breathtaking and beautiful*. I've always felt like it was a visible explanation to illustrate the buildup of emotions you experienced as a child. Just like a star, a heart can only handle so much pressure. It's not your fault. It's a balance of the natural world. It's unfathomable to think about what you went through." His eyes studied my face and then he added, "I would never judge you for anything you went through."

"You're saying I have a Super Nova heart?" There was awe in my tone as I was deeply touched by how gently and beautifully he had managed to describe my experience.

"Exactly like that." I swear Fulton was the only guy on the planet who can take a scientific explanation and make it romantic. He brushed a stray strand of hair behind my ear, letting his hand linger on my cheek. I wanted him to kiss me—and the heated look he gave me said that he also wanted to—but instead he leaned back, giving me more space. His pushback wasn't like a heart-stabbing thing though. It felt more like a shy timidness. Which I actually understood, because although we'd officially dated for months, we hadn't spent that much time being physically together as a couple. Other than one amazing week when he had come to visit me in Paris—which had been beyond anything I could have ever envisioned—as we got to share our first kiss in front of the Eiffel tower, just like in a movie. My memory made my face flush, and I missed the feelings I used to have for him as I recalled how we had so easily fell from friends to more than that. With defeated breath, I gave in, "So, how do I fix a Super Nova heart?"

The corners of his mouth lifted slightly. "You don't fix it. It's not broken. It balanced its way to a more beautiful existence."

I relented. At this point, I was mush. I never thought physics could be poetic or make me into a giant pile of putty, but his words barreled a path right to my heart. I was so ready to be over the drama, and I knew Fulton wasn't going anywhere. I had no idea what I did to deserve someone like him, but I was ready to forgive and give it another shot. "So . . . what do we do to fix us?"

Fulton's smiled sweetly at me. "We . . . we could dance." He was obviously trying to be cute, but it seemed played out. His grin lingered, waiting for me to accept his invitation and when I didn't, he softened his voice, "What's wrong?"

My whole life I had hid behind dance to avoid feeling but I didn't want dance to be my crutch at this point. I wanted something better, and I wasn't afraid to admit that anymore. "I don't want to dance with you because that's what I do to avoid." I tilted my head back and whispered into his ear, "I want a heart that knows how to dance."

He whispered back, "I know you do." Then without waiting for a cue from me, he wrapped his arm around my waist, pulling me closer to him and said, "Just wait until you see what a Super Nova heart can do . . ." Then his lips crashed down on mine, and like that we were pulled together, kissing each other like no time was lost. Fulton was back in my heart. Actually, I don't think he ever really left. He had just gotten temporarily camouflaged. Now that the dust had been settled, I saw him clearly and I excitedly looked forward to a future with him as I imagined all the dances a Super Nova heart could do . . .

Thank you for reading ***A Heart that Dances***. If you want to follow Abs on the final leg of her journey, you can read about it in ***A Heart that Loves.***

Also by J.P Sterling

Christmas Shenanigans (All Standalones)

Mingle All the Way

Tis the Season to Get Married

Let's Not and Sleigh We Did

The Coffee Loft Series (All Standalones)

Pardon My French Press

No More Mr. Chia Guy

Truly, Madly, Steeply Brew

Sweet Hockey RomCom (All Standalones)

The Pucker-Up Pact

Shot Through the Heart

Come and Get Your Glove (Coming 2025)

A Modern Fairy Tale Series (All Standalones)

Royally Rugged

Bosses and Billionaires Series (All Standalones)

Maid for my Billionaire Boss

Upcycling My Rig-Pig Boss

Kissed by My Billionaire Boss

Marooned with My Celebrity Boss

A Heart that Dances Series (A New Adult Series)

Dancing on Broken Ankles

The Stars We See

A Heart that Dances

A Heart that Loves

Water and Stone Duet (A coming-of-age Series)

Ruby in the Water

Lily in the Stone